# Retribution

## Avenge the Innocents

By

R.W.K. Clark

Published in the United States by Clarkltd.
Po Box 45313 Rio Rancho, NM 87174
info@clarkltd.com

Edition 1

United States Copyright Office
#1-7279683292 January 2019
Library of Congress Control Number:
2019900212
International Standard Book Numbers
ISBN-10: 1948312301
ISBN-13: 978-1948312301
ASIN: B07MC55YHN

/200801

# CONTENTS

# ACKNOWLEDGMENTS

I dedicate this novel to my wonderful readers and for all the amazing people I've met and those I haven't. To my family and loved ones, all your support will not be forgotten.

This book was made possible by reviews from readers like you.

Thank you

R.W.K. Clark

# CHAPTER 1

"Mommy, it's happening again…"

Marissa leaned her head over the edge of the ratty sofa where she had spent most of the last year heaving and gagging into the strategically placed mixing bowl on the floor beside her. For the next several minutes her tiny, pale body continued to wretch. Finally, nothing more would come up, but the heaving continued, wracking her body and bringing tears to her eyes that ran down her face like drops of rain. This exhausted the poor four-year-old, and when it finally stopped, she collapsed back onto her pillow, panting heavily. Covered in sweat and ashen in color, the little girl's eyes began to droop as she started to head back toward sleep.

Caroline Thomas, who had been in the kitchen, reached her daughter just as the bout ended and placed a cold, damp rag on the child's forehead. The medicine wasn't working, just as she knew it wouldn't. Neither had any of the other medications that had been prescribed for Marissa in the last twelve or so months, and she knew they wouldn't either. No one would listen to her, so she merely became more and more determined to prove that the doctors just didn't know what they were talking about.

"Marissa, is it over?" she asked softly. "Are you okay?"

The girl moaned and nodded slightly, then drifted off. Caroline studied her daughter: The child was almost entirely white, with the exception of the dark gray circles that had seemingly become permanent around her eyes. She was skin and bones, unable to hold anything down, including water. The last doctor, a disease specialist who had prescribed the previous round of medications, had threatened to hospitalize Marissa yet again if she didn't improve. That was precisely what Caroline wanted. Well, she didn't want the girl to die, for crying out loud. It was time to take her back to Dr. Fisher.

As she dressed and bundled her sleeping daughter, Caroline thought about their last visit to the Children's Health Center, where she had been taking Marissa for about three months. Prior to that, she had been seen at many locations; each one had successively referred them to the next, and they ended up with Dr. Fisher at CHC. At the last visit, he had told her he was going to research a few things and narrow down causes based on Marissa's surroundings, diet, and possible exposures. Since the girl had been out of preschool for nearly the entire year, and since she wasn't eating anything due to being ill, that left her surroundings.

Maneuvering her blanket-wrapped daughter in her arms, Caroline flung the huge pink diaper bag that served as both purse and medical record attaché over her shoulder. Once she got adjusted, she grabbed the keys to her rusty jalopy and headed out the apartment door. The landlady, Mrs. Fox, lived right across the hall, and she was the first face Caroline saw as she closed the door hard behind her.

"Oh, dear! Not again!" The elderly lady's concern and compassion were obvious on her face and in her voice. "I'll watch your place, Caroline. Heavens, could there be a better, more tolerant mommy than you?"

Caroline appeared to brush off the compliment, but in reality, she was reveling in it. "It is what a mother does when her child is sick; she doesn't have to think twice about it. You remember how it is."

Mrs. Fox followed her as quickly as her small legs would allow all the way to the stairs leading to the first floor, and the main entrance. "Is there anything else I can do for you? Call someone, perhaps?"

Caroline started down the stairs. "Mrs. Fox, you know there is no one." Suddenly, she paused and turned around to look at the woman when she was halfway down. "Wait, yes, there is. Could you call the Children's Health Center and tell them I am bringing Marissa Thomas in. She is having another attack; she has gotten worse. I forgot to phone them in a rush."

"Of course, dear," Mrs. Fox replied as Caroline rounded the corner to the second set of steps leading down and disappeared from sight. "You drive carefully, now. And keep me posted!"

Moments later, Caroline was speeding down the street on her way to CHC, her eyes darting from the road before her to her rearview mirror and back, over and over. Marissa was lying in a ball on the passenger seat, bouncing slightly as her mother drove, but she didn't move a muscle on her own, and she didn't utter a peep.

She turned onto the main drag without really stopping at the sign and glanced around hoping a cop had seen her, but there were none. Having a police escort was always exciting. The only problem was that the cop became the hero. They never failed to steal her thunder, but they got her seen immediately at every hospital she ever went to, and that was what she wanted. Caroline punched the gas and smiled.

∞

Herb Fisher had been a medical doctor specializing in pediatric disease for more than twenty-five years, and many of the ailments suffered by children he saw had set his teeth on edge. But this particular case, involving four-year-old Marissa did more, it left a horrible taste in his mouth and turned his stomach. Something was off, though he couldn't narrow it down. Fisher was getting closer, however. He promised himself that if her mother had to bring her in to see him again, he would let her know of his suspicions. But he would have to be very careful because if his suspicions were correct, he couldn't be sure what the mother would do. He had to have proof and to get proof, he had to know what he was trying to prove. Therein was where the problem lay.

"Ms. Thomas, I have to tell you that I am more than a bit baffled," the doctor began as he sat on a black swivel stool and leaned forward toward Caroline, his hands on his knees. The small hospital consultation room went quiet, then he spoke again. "For the symptoms that Marissa is showing, and the test results we have obtained over the past couple of months, the treatments we have administered, should have eradicated any issues. Instead, she is worse. So, I am recommending hospitalization immediately. This will give us time to conduct more thorough testing, and we can begin a nourishment program by administering a feeding tube."

He continued to talk, watching her face closely for any change in expression. She maintained perfect eye contact, looked deathly concerned, and nodded in agreement with all of his suggestions. This surprised Dr. Fisher because he suspected the girl was ill directly because of her mother. He expected the woman to get nervous or try to argue with hospitalizing her, but he got none of that. The girl needed to be in the hospital, he was saying; don't try to disagree with me on this one.

"I completely agree," Caroline conceded immediately as she forced a tear out of her left eye and allowed it to roll freely down her cheek. "I am simply at the end of my rope. Like I said, she seemed to be improving a couple of days after starting this last round of medication, but the next thing I knew she was throwing up worse than before, and she seems to be in a daze now most all of the time." The woman paused and broke into full tears. "I don't care what you have to do… just help me help my baby."

Dr. Fisher plucked a tissue from a box on the counter to his left and handed it to the woman. When she blew her nose on it, he grabbed the entire container and handed it over. While she tried to dry her tears he studied her harder. If she was the cause of the symptoms, as he had been beginning to suspect two appointments ago, she was indeed giving her best to convincing him otherwise. He began to doubt himself more than once just in the few minutes since the tears started to fall. Time to poke a bit harder at the bull.

He crossed his arms over his chest and, keeping his eyes on her, continued. "You know, Ms. Thomas, I have been doing some extra research especially for Marissa's case during my off hours. I don't mind telling you that I have lost sleep over it, and with you bringing her back today, I am sure to lose more. I was so hopeful that she would make a complete turnaround. I do have hope, however. During my research, I came across a couple of cases that are very similar to Marissa's."

"You mean you may have figured this horrible thing out?"

Wow, she was deceiving, Dr. Fisher thought. Well, honest or one of the evilest human beings on the face of the planet. The truth was, he hadn't figured anything out, he only suspected the things that it could be. The man was convinced that Marissa had been, or was being, poisoned. Whether or not it was accidental, he couldn't say. It was entirely possible that the girl had gotten into some dangerous household chemical and was continuing to do so. Or she had gotten into it once or twice, and the toxins did so much damage that the effects were now untreatable and irreversible. That was the reason he was treading so lightly; Caroline may, in fact, be a profoundly concerned mother who merely didn't have a clue.

But he genuinely doubted it for several reasons.

So, he had lied about the research. All he had really done was go over her records from every hospital and clinic she had gone to since this all began. He had pored over them again and again, and every last doctor and clinician who had contributed anything to her record had been stumped, just as he was. The difference for him came in the form of a memory, the memory of a boy of eight who had been a patient in 1972.

Fisher hadn't been his attending physician, but he had been one who cared for the boy during one of his stays at the hospital. He had been in several times with symptoms that were very similar to Marissa's: vomiting, diarrhea, weight loss, joint and muscle pain… the works. He was losing weight, and the ability to communicate was diminishing as well. During the stay that stood out in Fisher's mind, the boy was fading fast, and his life was only saved thanks to some fleeting genius in the lab who stumbled upon the cause. The boy would come in nearly at death's door, stay and get treatment for a few days, improve, and be sent home. A week later he would return, worse than before. This had happened several times, and the lab tech finally decided to go outside the boundaries of doctor's orders and checked him for poisoning. When the tech found cyanide, the mother got the blame. As it turned out, she had been obtaining the chemical from the local manufacturing plant, where she had a part-time job at night as a cleaning lady. She was taking small amounts home at a time and putting tiny doses in her husband's beer when he got back from work in the early afternoon. Turned out that he had been beating her since the moment she had said 'I do,' and he was beginning to show violence to the boy, which drove her over the edge. The solution she had come up with went all wrong for one reason: The boy, curious as all children are, had been sneaking sips of his dad's beer in an attempt to understand why dad got so mad when he drank it. The woman had not been too bright, however, coupled with a very immature personality and limited ability to reason. She hadn't been giving her husband enough of the chemical to do anything but make him slightly sick; for her son, however, it was proving to be enough to kill him if not for the lab tech who went the extra mile.

Now, here he sat with the mother of a child on the verge of death, and that boy and his case were the things his mind continued to go back to every time he pondered the sick Marissa. Up to this point, she had visited CHC a handful of times over the last two months or so, and the usual battery of tests had been done, but nothing outside of the ordinary. But upon seeing the mere shell of a girl once again, this time looking as though he had been so far off base it could cost him his ability to practice medicine, he began to take his earlier fleeting suspicions a bit more seriously. Something was going on here that felt and tasted ugly. He wanted her in the hospital where he could begin to check for the poisons that were commonly used to kill. He didn't want to find any, and he certainly didn't want to think that a mother could do something like poison her child, but he had to check everything if he wanted to be able to live with himself.

"I'm glad you're in agreement, Ms. Thomas." Fisher relaxed a bit on the stool, crossed one leg over the other, and turned on the stool to face the lowered part of the counter that served as a desk. He flipped open Marissa's file and with the click of a pen, began to write furiously on a sheet of paper inside. "I'm going to have her admitted immediately. There are a couple of things, in particular, I am looking for, but I need to ask you a couple of questions first. Your answers may help narrow things down better since no one has looked in this direction before."

"Absolutely, Doctor."

He turned to her, pen poised over the file. "Do you live in a house or an apartment?"

"Apartment… it's in a six-plex over on Beekman Avenue."

"How long have you lived there?"

Caroline shifted in her chair, and to Fisher, she looked like she was relaxing a bit. "Um, just about two years."

"Are you aware of any problems with pests in the building?" he asked.

"Pests?"

Fisher nodded. "Yes, pests. Rats, roaches, etc."

Caroline immediately shook her head. "No, nothing like that. Mrs. Fox… she's our landlady… takes outstanding care of the grounds and the units. I've never seen, or even heard rumors about anything like that."

The doctor scribbled on the paper and continued. "How about playmates? Does Marissa have any little friends who she visits with to play? Or perhaps relatives who she may visit?" He stopped and looked at her. "Is there any place she goes that may have a problem with pests?"

"Not that I'm aware of."

He wrote for a few moments more, then picked up the receiver of the telephone on the small countertop. After punching in only four numbers, he spoke into the phone.

"Jeanette, we are going to be admitting Marissa Ann Thomas immediately. I would like her placed in a private room, if possible. If we have none immediately available, rearrange things, so there is one. I don't care what you have to do; until we have a firmer grip on the cause of her condition, we cannot run the risk of having her with the other children. Yes, yes, put her under partial quarantine. No, no special precautions on the part of medical staff. No, no, don't worry about running any tests right away; I'll put in orders for what I specifically want once she is settled in. Yes. Thank you."

He hung up the phone, wrote some more chicken

scratch in Marissa's file, then closed it and turned entirely to Caroline. "I'm going to change the focus a bit as far as approaching a correct diagnosis. I think Marissa may have had an opportunity to get some type of poison into her system, and that may be the cause of all this."

"Poison?" Caroline's heart was thumping so hard now she could have sworn it was audible to the doctor. "What kind of poison?"

The man shrugged slightly. "There are several types of poisoning that she could be suffering from that result from inadvertent contact with various household products… products common for everyday use. I'm going to have the lab run the gamut; in other words, we'll check for cyanide, arsenic, strychnine and the like. Those are chemicals that Marissa could have gotten ahold of without even being aware of what she had; you would have been oblivious as well."

Dr. Fisher noted that Caroline calmed significantly at that point. Maybe she wasn't guilty of any wrongdoing, but the fact remained that she shouldn't have relaxed so quickly unless there was something he was missing, something she was glad he had ignored. What had he overlooked? Anything? Maybe it was all in his mind.

"Well, I think the sooner we get this ball rolling, the better. Thank you so much, Doctor. Can I go to Marissa now?"

With that, the pair returned to the room where Marissa was being monitored by a nurse who was reading a fashion magazine while the child slept. Within thirty minutes she was moved to a private room with only a couple of watercolor paintings of zoo animals on the walls and a hard vinyl chair. Once she was settled, Dr. Fisher, who had already ordered an IV for re-hydration, went ahead and put through an order for blood and urine tests, most bearing letters for names that Caroline didn't completely understand.

"It will be wonderful if you find something concrete this time, Doctor," she said. "It seems like so long ago she was healthy and playful. I can hardly remember what it's like to get a good night's sleep without watching and worrying about her throwing up or worse… not waking at all. You don't know what it will mean to me."

Dr. Fisher was writing in Marissa's file furiously once again. "I can imagine that it has been terribly difficult for both of you. This is just a theory I have; I am hopeful that it will show us something and we can stop this once and for all. That is really all we have at this point: hope. Just hold on to that and know that no matter what…" Fisher closed Marissa's chart with a snap and hung it on the foot of her bed. "I will not quit until something is known, and we take appropriate action."

Caroline fought the urge to follow the chart with her eyes. "Thank you, Doctor."

"You should eat something or get out for some fresh air. A lab tech and a couple of nurses will be coming in soon to take blood and catheterize her for urine; I doubt Marissa will be able to give them a sample herself, for obvious reasons." Fisher's eyes were glued to her as he spoke.

R.W.K. Clark

# CHAPTER 2

Marissa's mother smugly bundled her weak, dying body into her car that day. She had known varying degrees of sickness and pain most of the mere handful of days that made up her life to that point. Even at that tender age, she was aware, somewhere deep inside of her body, that something just wasn't right. She hardly knew a day of wellness, and the ones she could recall paled next to the vast number of sick ones.

Marissa also knew that she was going to die from it. She couldn't have explained how she knew; the truth was that she really had no grasp on what it meant to 'die.' It was only a word she had heard, both from people around her and on television; it had no real meaning at all. She thought about the word, people always seemed to say it when they were crying or angry. The picture that formed in her small, young, innocent brain resembled more a full-color photo of a birthday party during vacation than a sorrow-filled funeral wake in black and white. She was so sick, so much of the time that little Marissa couldn't wait to go die, even if it did make her mommy yell or cry herself to sleep.

She loved her mommy like nobody else she had ever

met in her short life. When she looked at Caroline she saw sunlight and perfection; her eyes were as blue as the sky when there were no clouds in it, and her reddish-blond hair seemed to sparkle when it was shiny, like glitter. But Marissa had inspected her mommy's hair up close with the lamp shining on it, and there was no glitter. Marissa could see that it was nothing more than an illusion created by the light and the shiny spots in her hair. Caroline would let her brush it sometimes, and she would take her time running the brush through it, in long, straight strokes from scalp to hair's end, over and over. She would watch the sparkles in mommy's hair, and for some reason they always made her get stinging tears in her eyes, and she would feel sad for no reason. Marissa didn't understand that, either.

All she knew anymore, was that her tummy hurt all the time, and she was hungry... so hungry! But when she would eat food it would throw itself up out of her stomach hard, and her belly would be so mad about it that it would keep trying to throw up, but there was no more food or drinks in there. She felt tired all the time.

She just knew that every time she stayed in the hospital she felt better, and her food stayed in her tummy where it belonged. But then mommy would take her home after she stayed some nights with the nurses, and by the very next day she would throw up again.

It had gotten so bad that it wore the little preschooler out just to lift her head for a drink; it literally took all of her energy and breath.

She hoped she got to 'die' soon. After she had dry

heaved in the living room of the small, two-bedroom apartment she lived in with her mommy, her throat got so sore she could barely swallow at all. She wanted water, crisp and cold and clean, but every time she was able to drink without being sick, mommy always wanted to give her flavored drink mix. When Marissa thought about any flavor of the drink mix her stomach threatened to heave almost right away. She used to like it, and now she wished they would flush away every last drop on the planet.

∞

While she slept, a nearly-hollow shell of a body that almost disappeared entirely beneath the warmed-up blankets on her hospital bed, she dreamed of being angry. She was mad, so crazy that she growled and spit and clawed. The thing wanted to get her, and she always put up a good fight, running and kicking and scratching. But the evil was more substantial than she; it continuously caught her, and it always laughed when it did.

The thing was black, and it didn't look like anybody, but most of all it didn't look like a person. It was always smiling and licking its lips while she screamed and cried, and Marissa knew the thing was terrible. It had legs, but never seemed to use them when pursuing her; the malevolence was always right behind her, no matter how fast she ran, and no matter how hard she cried.

It had the shape of a person, but it was all things yucky and rotten. The malice was made of black goop, and sometimes, when Marissa looked over her shoulder while she was running from it, she would see globs of its body dripping off its chin or dangling from its elbow in great drops, which would hit the ground with a light, wet 'splat!'… that yucky, bad old thing was falling apart. Marissa was sure it was because the thing liked to cause hurt.

She knew the thing thoroughly, had endured nights filled with the horror for as long as she could remember, but she was too little to make it stop coming. When she slept, and in the dreams, she was too small to fight it away or outrun it. In her visions, she was just the size of an ant, and the thing chased her, casting her into pitch black as she ran and cried. The shadow of it was as big as the sky, as big as the moon, as big as mommy.

∞

Marissa had started to draw back from interacting socially when she was four. Nothing she could pretend with her playmates was going to help them have fun; it was all hospitals and doctors. The other girls at school were afraid of getting sick from being around Marissa, and understandably so, but most of all they didn't want to play with her because by the time they were finished they always felt sad. None of the tiny children understood it, and they were still too young to be catty or bully towards Marissa because of their confusion. All they knew was that when they played with Marissa, some of the things she wanted them to pretend about just didn't sound right, and it made them feel weird. She wanted to be the mom, and she always wanted her kid to be really sick like she constantly was, but worst of all, she always wanted to force them to drink lots of flavored drink mix. Marissa didn't like it, but all the healthy kids did.

So, subconsciously, and with no ill-will or nastiness, the other girls in her class slowly began to drift away, so slowly that they still trickled in and out of Marissa's playtime life for several days, but they would always find something to rush off to. It wasn't the first time, though, so she thought she was used to it. It happened everywhere they lived, and since her daddy didn't live with them anymore, Marissa and mommy lived in a lot of different places. She had been pushed away constantly, so the solution she chose was to stay away from them and try her best to not feel lonely.

R.W.K. Clark

# CHAPTER 3

She had been lying still on the hospital bed, eyes closed tight, little back to the door. Had mommy gone home for good? Marissa sure hoped so. As much as she loved her mommy, this sickness was getting hard. She wanted to hurry up and feel better at this hospital. Being sick this time was getting so bad that Marissa couldn't think right, her mind was jumbled and confused. She wasn't sure if she was sleeping or awake. The more time she was at the hospital with Dr. Fisher and the nurses the better her body would feel, and she could hardly wait.

So, Marissa was under those blankets, curled up in a ball with her arms wrapped protectively around her legs, and her eyes squeezed shut. She kept herself busy in the sanitary silence by thinking, which consisted of fantasizing about running across a grass field at full speed, the wind in her hair and the sun on her face. Behind her were other girls, all running, all from different daycares or preschools, each being someone Marissa thought was her friend, but in the end disappeared, just like everything in life so far… just like everyone in her life had.

Everyone but her mommy, who she thought she must be 'allergic' to. After all, something about mommy was making her sick. Either that or she finally got 'allergic' to flavored drink mix.

Suddenly the doorknob on her room door turned and gave a slightly muffled metallic clank as it released itself from the jamb and opened inward. Marissa jumped in spite of continually listening for any and every noise heading to whatever space she was occupying in the universe. She was always looking... for mommy's voice or steps, so she could make her breathing go slow and get ready to hear about how sick she was, and why she has to have the awful drink mix. She was listening for doctors or nurses to come and tell her they knew that something at home was making her sick, that they didn't know what it was, but she never had to go back there until they figured it out. Busy listening for a voice telling her that she had a new mom and dad that would never make her lie in a bed all the time and drink flavors with too much sugar. She wished for her dad, who was going to take her to live with him.

"Marissa? Marissa honey, are you awake?"

She had been holding her breath under that blanket, and she didn't even know it. As soon as she heard the smooth, youthful voice belonging to one of the pretty nurses, she knew it wasn't mommy, and she could let herself breath again. Slowly, so slowly, Marissa released the air out of her lungs, then slowly began to breathe as frequently as her worn out body would allow.

"Yes," she replied, her voice crackly and weak. She

tried to roll over onto her back, but her frail little arm couldn't even push her body over. "I was just having dreams."

Suddenly the nurse was behind her. Gently, she helped the sickly girl onto her back. She fluffed Marissa's pillow and carefully replaced it, then asked if she wanted fresh warm blankets. Marissa had smiled and nodded, shyness coming over her entire body. She tried to cover her head, but it wasn't happening.

The nurse left the room and returned with two blankets, fresh from the warmer. After getting rid of the cool ones and covering the girl back up, the nurse poured a cup of cold water and sat on the edge of Marissa's bed. She helped the shaking girl drink, only letting her get a couple of sips. They wanted to make sure it was going to stay down.

"What's your name?" Marissa asked the nurse in a voice that was just above a whisper. She had the blankets pulled up to her nose, and her sharp blue eyes peered warily over the edges.

The nurse smiled down at Marissa as she crossed her legs and set the water cup on the nightstand. "I'm Nurse Jennings, but you should call me Trish. I just got on an hour ago, so I'll be here with you for the rest of the night." The woman studied her patient, who seemed to be nothing more than death-warmed-over. "So, I was wondering if you noticed that the doctor had us put an IV in."

Marissa nodded. "Why are you letting me have water if I have an IV? Mommy says I'm not 'posed to, that it's too much for my tummy." A sad look came over her face, then just as quickly, her smile returned, lighting up her eyes. "That water was so good!" Marissa giggled, barely noticing that she didn't feel like throwing up at all. She wasn't even all hot and sweaty and smelly.

"You like water? Wow! Most of the kids don't want to drink it, so they must have an IV. I think that's why Dr. Fisher had us give it to you; he was worried you wouldn't be able to take water, or that you wouldn't want it. Most kids want soda or juice, or lots of flavored drink mix. What do you like best?"

Marissa's smile disappeared quickly, and the tension that came to her body was evident right away, even under the blankets. "I hate drink mix!"

Her passion and instant anger made Trish Jennings jump slightly, startled by the change in Marissa's demeanor. And it was triggered, instantly, by the mere mention of flavored drink mix? This was the type of thing Dr. Fisher had ordered her to be listening and looking for. He didn't tell them he was suspicious, but the nurses had put it together on their own. They knew what to look for, even though they couldn't fathom the act Caroline Thomas was suspected of.

"Well, Marissa, I can promise you that you won't see a drop of that while you're here," Trish replied softly, a look of love and compassion on her face. "Not unless you ask for it on purpose."

"I never will."

Trish nodded. "Would you like some more water, though? Just another sip or two? You seem to be holding the last ones down." She helped the girl drink, then put the cup back on the nightstand. "How are you feeling?"

The girl gave a playful groan, which she exaggerated slightly for an effect like it was all so burdensome. It was, but it was a game she played, letting the nurses and doctors see the real Marissa, the one who liked to tease and play. Someday one of them would think she was too funny. They would love how she made them all laugh like crazy, and they would take her home with them and their family forever.

"So much better." She stared up into Trish's eyes, which were large and brown, and they had the longest, prettiest eyelashes Marissa had ever seen. "I thought that I was going to die when my tummy was trying to throw out stuff that wasn't in there earlier. I couldn't even think, I was so sick. Now I feel pretty good. Trish, your eyes are so big and brown."

The young nurse flushed, and she tried to maintain her focus as she dug a small, pocket-sized spiral notebook out of her smock top. She jotted down 'drink mix,' then tensed up immediately and seemed repulsed by the thought.

"How long since my mommy left?"

Trish glanced up at a large white clock on the wall over the door that had big black hands and numbers. "Oh, my!" Her voice was filled with exaggeration as she tried to make the child smile. "It is nearly three o'clock in the morning, Marissa! Aren't you feeling tired?"

As if on cue, Marissa opened her mouth wide and

yawned for what seemed like an eternity. When she was finished, her eyes drooped slightly, and she gave a weak nod. Her eyes were fastened on Trish's, and the young nurse waited patiently to start tucking the girl in; she sensed that Marissa wanted to speak, and sure enough, she did.

"I'm happy I'm here so the doctor can make me better again," she said in a timid, almost whispered, tone. "I'm tired of being sick. Someday I want to make some friends."

It was all Trish could do to keep her tears in check. With a quick, but reaffirming nod, she stood and began to straighten and adjust Marissa's blankets. "They are cooling off, so if you get cold just push your button, and one of us will get here right away to fetch some fresh ones for you, okay?" She made sure the side guards were raised and locked properly in place before she rested her elbows on them and gazed down at the pale child on the mattress. "Promise me you'll try to eat some breakfast when they bring it to you, if I'm not here, that is. Promise?"

Marissa nodded, and Trish noticed that the girl was holding something back. "What? What is it, Marissa?"

With a shrug, the child hesitantly replied, "But the faster I get better, the quicker they send me home, and I always get sick at home, Trish. I don't want to go home."

Now the tears threatened to come full-force, and Trish had to quickly turn away. She opted to grab the child's chart and pretend to be reading it, that way

Marissa wouldn't see the rage and pain on her face. She wanted to do something drastic to Caroline Thomas, something to stop her from continuing to murder her own daughter. All she could do was watch and wait, it was the only option she had.

After a moment she turned back to Marissa and tucked her in. Marissa was worn out from their brief interaction, and all Trish wanted was for the girl to rest and recover. But at the same time, they would just send her home to be made sick again. Trish wanted to call the police or social services. But procedures had to be followed, or evidence and documentation would be lost. The next thing anyone would know would be that Caroline Thomas had disappeared and she had taken the victim of her rampage with her.

Marissa was sleeping before the tucking was finished, so Trish tidied up the few scant belongings that sat on the adjustable bed table and pushed it up against the wall and out of the way. She stood, motionless, just staring at Marissa's sleeping face for the longest time before conceding to the fact that she couldn't protect the child every second; she was safe right there and right then, and that was all that was in Trish's or any of the other nurses' control.

Closing the door gently, as so it wouldn't shut loudly, she left the room, inhaled deeply, and made her way to the next one.

R.W.K. Clark

# CHAPTER 4

For most, the darkness would have been not only tangible but painful and panic-inducing. It enveloped those within it and took over all their senses until the lack of stimuli or the sheer hopelessness of it threatened to drive them to madness. To her, though, the darkness was comforting. It helped to close out the world and the troubles in it, resulting in peace and clarity.

The only light in the room was the intermittent glowing of the end of her cigarette, which she pulled on about every twenty seconds or so. Her eyes were wide and dilated in an effort to see her surroundings. Blackness with amusing shooting embers that were nothing more than tiny illusions gleaming about before her were all she could see. She chuckled softly to herself briefly before stifling a sob of futility and dread. It had come down to it again; she had always known it would.

She was tired of flitting about with her child and possessions. If only someone, anyone, would give her the recognition and appreciation she deserved. Then and only then would all of this stop. It was so painful, having no family, no real friends, and no man in her life on any kind of regular basis. If someone loved her the way they ought to she could be free of the cycle, she seemed to be caught up in.

But it wasn't a cycle... not really. It was nothing more than a repeat of lessons that those outside of herself needed to learn. One experience, really. That she was human, and she deserved to be given credit for the terribly tricky life she was living, the immensely crappy hand she had been dealt. She would get that validation before it was over.

A voice in the back of her head nagged, and she fought with it periodically, beating it down to mere silence. It suffocated and infuriated her with its incessant droning. Sometimes, when she couldn't beat it down, she would have to take something to shut it up. More than once this method of squashing the voice had proven to be more trouble than it was worth, nearly killing her or someone around her. No, drinking or taking a pill was not preferable because she could never maintain control of her emotions or self when she used them. Instead, she would fight the voice until it succumbed, only to pop back into her head at the most unwanted opportunity.

It told her she was killing her baby, that if she kept it up, she would not only ruin the child but end her life entirely. She thought of her daughter Marissa's perfect little face, so angelic and beautiful. Did Marissa deserve to be ill all the time? When was the last time she had been out to play, like the other kids in the neighborhood, or even felt well enough to participate in classroom activities with others in her class? The woman couldn't remember. She was the cause… it was plain and simple. There was no denying it.

"Well, God should get moving then and get someone to love me. Marissa wouldn't have to suffer at all if He would just do His job." Her voice was monotonous, and the utter darkness made it sound even duller and more lifeless.

Marissa loves you already, the voice pressured. The one that loves you truly and unconditionally is the one you are killing.

Immediately, Caroline opened her mouth and let out a shrill scream. It was a scream without hope and filled with rage. As she screamed, she could almost visualize the voice as it vanished away in horror at having pushed her so far. This thought made her scream even more loudly, loud enough to drown out the sound of her neighbor's voices out in the hallway speaking of where such a cry could be coming from. She screamed and screamed until someone dared to take their knuckles and rap hard at her apartment door.

"Miss Thomas? Miss Thomas, are you in there? Is everything alright?"

Her screaming stopped as quickly as it had started. It had been Mrs. Fox's voice, she was sure of it. Even as she sat there holding her breath, she could hear the neighbors mumbling with the landlady in the hall. She wanted to grab each of them by their indignant necks and squeeze until their ugly heads popped off.

"Caroline?"

She suddenly flopped forward from where she sat

on the sofa and buried her face in a pillow, so she could breathe. They would hear her for sure, taking in a breath and breathing so carelessly. She had to keep them away; they all wanted to take what was hers: her daughter. She was sure each and every one of them was suspicious of what she was doing to Marissa when no one was looking.

She wanted to die.

Enough! She screamed at herself in her mind. There was no time for panic or any other useless emotion. She listened carefully to the voices until they dwindled to silence, each one heading back to their own living space. Like any of them gave two shits about her, she thought.

It was time to really think things through and take back control of the situation that God's laziness was creating.

∞

Her mind went back to the meeting with Dr. Fisher. It left butterflies in her stomach because Caroline knew exactly why Marissa was so ill. She just wasn't telling.

Caroline looked the perfect picture of a mother worn out and worried sick in a panic for her ill child, but inside she was calm, cool, and collected. Marissa would be okay; she knew when to ease up and when to stop. She had the whole game down to a fine art.

What Dr. Fisher didn't know was that while Caroline was putting her pretenses on full display, her mind was far from the small hospital consultation room. She was worried, but at the same time she was enjoying the excitement of the risk and soaking up the fact that this man was giving her his full attention. Was he on to her, she wondered? No, he was acting like he should be: a physician who was stumped and completely worried about the child in his care and her life. He showed all the right signs: leaning forward to let her know how dangerous the situation was, creasing his forehead and keeping one eyebrow raised, and most of all, enunciating particular words to drive them home.

Just like that, Caroline heard the red flag words she had heard several times before from other doctors at other hospitals. They were the words that told her they were getting too close to figuring things out, and she was playing a perilous game. She didn't flinch or change her expression from concern to fear. Instead, she ignored the trembling in her stomach and the pick-up in her heartbeat and feigned excitement.

Caroline's heart was pounding, but she maintained her façade of eager relief that 'finally someone was going to do something.' She would listen to his questions and answer them honestly unless she sensed any suspicion aimed in her direction. Then she would do as she had done before: skillfully turn everything around like the master manipulator she was.

It worried her, and right away she began to bargain with God in her head. Let me get out of this one, and I'm done, she told Him. I'm not trying to hurt her, you know that. I just want someone to recognize how on top of things I am with Marissa. Lord, just get me out of this… I know I've been doing wrong. I won't do it anymore.

Dr. Fisher was insinuating she leave Marissa and go, as she looked up at him wiping at an invisible tear with a forefinger and forcing a smile. With a weak nod and smile, she agreed, but not before offering up reasons why she should stay for a while and then listening to him shoot them down. She had the feeling that if she continued to argue he would begin to get even more suspicious than he already was, and she knew from past experience that he was, indeed, suspicious. He acted the way they all did when things began to unravel: trying to insinuate he blamed the child's ignorance and didn't think mommy was involved, trying to appear to be her best friend with a soft voice uttering supportive words but staring at her with eyes of steel and full of paranoia. Yes, if she got out of this, she was going to stop.

As she left the room to go to the small cafeteria, Caroline thought of the plastic jug of automotive antifreeze in the trunk of her car and let out a long sigh. It would probably be alright this time. She would probably get away with it, but she had to stop before the time came that she didn't.

∞

Suddenly something stung the inner forefinger of Caroline's right hand. It took her by surprise and she jerked involuntarily. Out of the corner of her eye she watched the last remnants of a glowing cigarette coal take to the air, burn out, and land on the floor. There was no burning smell, so she merely chuckled at having forgotten the cigarette before popping her finger into her mouth to alleviate the sting of the burn. As she sucked on her finger, she let her mind wander to the beginning of the mess she had created.

James had been kind to her from the moment they first met. He had been the class 'bad boy' at her high school. She was the daughter of a pediatrician and his homemaker wife, both of whom were very high pressure and overly critical when it came to their only child. She had been unhappy for a very long time and was extremely introverted, but meeting James Thomas had changed all that. Before she knew it, she and her new boyfriend had gained reputations as the 'partiers' in school. Caroline didn't care about appearances like her mother and father did. Instead, she only cared about doing and being whatever made James happy.

Then she turned up pregnant, and he had been so happy. They both quit school and James got a job pumping gas at Richter's Petrol on the outskirts of town. It didn't take long for her parents to realize that she was with child, and they promptly gave her an ultimatum: leave James or get kicked out of the family house and onto the street. James' first paycheck went to renting them a room where they shared a bathroom with other tenants but had their own kitchenette.

They got married by the justice of the peace when Caroline was seven months along, and she couldn't have been happier. She couldn't wait until they were decent and stable on their feet so she could rub her parents' complaints and dissatisfaction in their uptight faces, but as soon as Marissa was born, something changed. Though she worshipped her young husband and catered to his every whim, he grew unhappy just as her parents had. He got home later and later from work, and when he did arrive, he would be half-drunk by the time he got there. Before long Caroline had enough and began to voice her opinion about his strange behavior.

At first, he objectively denied any wrongdoing and told her he was under a lot of stress at work. But when things continued to get worse, and she spoke up even more loudly, he started getting sick and tired of the sound of her voice. He complained that their place was a mess, that she was lazy, and that her mothering skills were sadly lacking. His words cut her to the bone, and before she knew it, Caroline was drawing back inside of herself, trying to think up ways to win back James' love.

She hadn't known that he was having an affair with a cash register girl at Richter's. The thought of him being guilty of infidelity had never entered her mind. She stooped to insane lows to win his love. While she did those things, he laughed to himself at her pathetic displays, feeling entertained by the humility of the woman who had borne his daughter.

Then, one day, she decided to take James his lunch at Richter's to surprise him. No one was at the pumps; the place was dead. As she had approached the building to go through the front door, she saw them through the paned glass window, kissing like crazy while James ran his hands hungrily up and down the strange girl's body.

Blindly, Caroline had run away. When James got home three hours late, she came unglued and began screaming, crying, and throwing accusations at him while the baby cried from her second-hand bassinet. James swung on her with an open hand, and as soon as the palm connected with the soft flesh of her cheek, sending her flying, he lost all control. He straddled her body and began hitting her over and over until her face was nothing but bloody bruises, and her left eye was swollen shut. While he hit her, he told her how much he hated her, how she lacked in every department, how she wasn't good enough and never would be, but she had trapped him, and he wouldn't be trapped!

James had stormed out of the apartment, and Caroline had cried herself to sleep that night. He had returned in the wee hours, and Caroline had woken up to him next to her on the bed, his back to her and his daughter. She watched him sleep for a while before bundling up Marissa and taking her in the stroller to the basement of the apartment building, where residents were able to store things in locked cages. She had seen what she was looking for down there before, and she knew right where to go.

Her parents had used rat poison before, one time, at her childhood residence when an old nearby home had been demolished and a nest of rats took to the neighboring houses. Her father had given her a long, educational lecture on the importance of never touching the stuff; he had driven home how terribly dangerous it was to human beings, and she should never even move the box it came in. Caroline had always wondered if it was as volatile as he had warned; today was the day she would find out.

So, back in the tiny apartment, she cleaned herself up and set about her day as if she hadn't endured a horrible beating by the man who was supposed to be her lover and protector. She cooked him a big breakfast with hot coffee spiked with strychnine, and she watched him eat and drink out of the corner of her eye so she could be on top of refilling his cup promptly. By the end of the day, the son of a bitch was home from work early rather than late, sick as a dog and twice as filthy. Instead of showering, he had spent the rest of the afternoon and evening intermittently sleeping and puking, and she had relished every moment of it.

It took him all of ten hours total to die; he had been a healthy young man. But die he did, and he did it right there in that tiny apartment on the bed. Caroline waited until the middle of the night and shoved his body out the window, where it landed in a large green dumpster down below in the alley. She had closed the window, locked it, and proceeded to call the police at 11:16 that night to report her husband missing. The responding officers clucked their tongues over her swollen face as she told them about the fight, and how he had never come home after storming out the night before when her beating was complete. More than likely he had gotten drunk and passed out at the woman's house whom he was seeing, police said. They would investigate, they promised, and let her know as soon as they had learned anything.

Caroline never called to follow up, James' body was never found, and the police investigation was forgotten.

Ultimately, nobody missed James, and she was finally free. But he wasn't the only thing to imprison her and cause her pain. Little did Caroline know that her illness was just beginning. Her mind would prove itself a much, much harsher master.

R.W.K. Clark

# CHAPTER 5

Caroline brought herself back to reality after countless minutes of pondering the past and the only man she ever loved. With a rapid shake of her head, she turned the lamp on next to the sofa, illuminating the darkness and sending her eyeballs into shock. Squinting, she ignored the pain and lit up a cigarette from her pack on the end table.

James never cared about her or Marissa anyway. Caroline was the best thing for the girl, and everything she had done was for their little two-person family. It would bring her the satisfaction of people seeing Caroline's worth, and maybe someday she would find the man who would love her and her daughter forever.

In the meantime, she needed to think. She needed to go over the regular plan used when she had come to the end of the line with a hospital. It was time to pack up and move on.

∞

The actual poisoning began when little Marissa was eleven months old, but the distancing and isolation commenced pretty much the moment her father 'left' for good.

Most of the time Caroline saw nothing but James when she looked at the daughter they had created together. Did she love the child? Yes, she had a love for her baby. Did she want to punish the little girl because of her father's behavior? Absolutely! Did the baby deserve to have the responsibility of making things right placed upon her small shoulders? Well, Caroline believed in a sick, twisted way that she did.

So, she mothered her, and then tried to kill her, and then cherished her all over again. Now, if others knew the truth about the situation, they would believe that Caroline totally deserved to die herself... they just didn't understand what she was doing. It had a purpose and meaning, and it was being brought to completion through the experience.

The truth of the matter was that Caroline didn't know what she would do without tiny Marissa acting as her 'crutch' and the very thought made her tremble with apprehension and shake full-on with fear. Marissa was her lifeline, her sole ability to communicate with the outside world, the world she had never fit into properly. Both of them were lost.

Here Caroline sat, just thinking about everything and determining her next move. Marissa was at the hospital and Caroline was in self-induced isolation on the sofa, inside their tiny apartment. The place she was in was not unfamiliar... the fact that she was responsible and must get them out of the mess they were in was something she had accepted from the very beginning. This was something she recognized from the very first dose.

Now she didn't use strychnine or any other careless tool. Different types of poison were risky, and you didn't have as much control. But ethylene glycol was something the user could get a good handle on, something she could plan with, and administer as she saw fit for the situation. If she wanted to use just a tad, just enough to make the intended just mildly ill, she could do it effortlessly. If she wanted to move things along at a faster pace, because she planned to kill, that was easy too. But if she just wanted to have someone ill on an even keel, without killing them, but enough to convince those around the intended that they, needed medical attention, well, that was the easiest of them all.

The best thing about that particular poison was that she didn't have to sign for it at a fish store or explain herself to a hardware man about having an aversion to rodents. She could readily go to the nearest quick mart and find it, ready and waiting, in a jug, prepared just for cooling a vehicle or keeping it from freezing.

She had read about ethylene glycol in an article in one of James' Mechanics Magazines. She read the article and then proceeded to try it out on a stray mongrel that roamed around in their low-income neighborhood. She spiked the canine's water with it, offered him chopped bologna, and then watched. Over the course of two weeks and much study and record keeping, the creature had died, right outside her back door. She perfected her technique by practicing on other animals, which satisfied Caroline that she had the dosing perfect.

Suddenly, the telephone rang shrilly from her right, jerking her out of her reverie violently, and Caroline growled at the object as if it were a spider or scorpion preparing to attack. She stared at it as it rang two more times, then reached out with animosity and picked it up.

"Hello?" she snapped.

"Mrs. Thomas?" The voice on the other end of the line sounded professional and curt, yet polite.

She paused. "This is Caroline Thomas."

"Hello, ma'am. This is Nurse Kelly at the Hospital. I'm calling to let you know that Dr. Fisher has given consent for Marissa to be released to go home. He would like to meet with you to give you care instructions prior to letting her go. Is there a time that is good for you?"

Caroline arched an eyebrow in the dark, curtain-shaded living room. Why would they be calling her in the middle of the night? Why would they be releasing Marissa at all hours?

"You want to send her home in the middle of the night? She's only been there for a day; how could she possibly be well?" Caroline was confused and paranoid, the primary thought in her mind is that they had things figured out and wanted to arrest her as soon as she got there… it was a setup.

There was a long moment of hesitation on the other end of the line, and Caroline got a clear sense of confusion from the silence. She waited a bit for the nurse to speak. Then, just as she opened her mouth to goad the woman into a response, the nurse answered.

"Mrs. Thomas, Marissa has been here for six days. You were here two days ago and spoke with Nurse Jennings." The woman waited a short second for a response but then continued. "Don't you remember? She told you Marissa was improving greatly and would likely be able to leave soon. Dr. Fisher is ready to release her, but he would like to meet with you first."

"Six... six days?"

There was definitely something time-wise that was not matching up with Caroline's recollections of the last week or so. The last thing she clearly remembered that involved little Marissa took place the day after she was admitted at CHC. She had delivered her daughter some books and her favorite toy, as a matter of fact. How could this woman say she had been there six days?

"But..."

"Yes, ma'am. Six days. She has been asking about you, about what time you will be coming to get her." The nurse cleared her throat tersely, and Caroline didn't miss the fact that her voice had gone from warm to freezing in seconds. "And as I said, Dr. Fisher wants to meet with you to discuss test results and how to best see to it that she is successful in her recovery once she is home."

Caroline narrowed her eyes as she listened to the woman. She couldn't be sure, but the woman sounded like what she was saying was legitimate. Her tone was calm, unquestionable, but that could just be her disposition. Well, it didn't matter anyway, she had to go pick the girl up if she was ready to be discharged. She had done it so many times before that it shouldn't be a problem. Besides, if they were going to arrest her, if Dr. Fisher had discovered something abnormal, there was nothing she could do about it. To not pick her daughter up would send up red flags for sure.

"Um, I'm sorry." Caroline chuckled and feigned embarrassment. "I was napping, and I guess I'm not all the way awake. When do I need to be there?"

The nurse immediately sounded more relaxed, and she even chuckled in return. "I understand, Mrs. Thomas. Just get here as soon as you can. I'm sure the doctor will understand as well. Having a sick child can take a lot out of a person."

"Fine," she replied. "I'll be there shortly. Thank you for the call."

"Of course. We'll see you soon then."

Caroline smirked in the darkness. "Yes. Oh, and please refer to me as Ms. Thomas in the future. I'm not married."

She hung up the phone without hesitation and sat smiling at her own boldness, leaving the young nurse stunned, staring at the telephone receiver in her hand. What a rude woman, Nurse Kelly thought. No wonder everyone thought she was the reason little Marissa was sick. Could one even imagine living with such a person? And she didn't even know what day it was.

The nurse hung up the phone and went to tell Dr. Fisher that Ms. Thomas would be on her way in, then she would get Marissa ready for discharge.

# CHAPTER 6

## A Rebellious Teen

Marissa put her foot down regarding what her mother was doing to her since she was nearly one. It had not been pretty, especially after she had allowed the woman to practically kill her over and over again. In her mother's sick mind, the near killing was not recognized. Caroline only saw the fact that she had saved her daughter repeatedly.

This time at the age of thirteen, they released Marissa from the Hospital, but just barely. As a matter of fact, they were calling Child Protective Services in on the day of her release to begin investigation and supervision, but her mother had snuck her out of her room. They then moved away as usual.

Shortly after settling in her mother made her a pitcher of flavored drink mix, and she put her foot down.

"No!" She had screamed, her thirteen-year-old body standing up in defiance, a fist held out before her mother's face. "It's over. If you want to make someone ill, do it to yourself. I'm done, and I'm going to start to live!"

Mommy Dearest had been furious, laying guilt trips and accusations that Marissa was just like her father, but the girl didn't take the bait. She purely refused and began to go about living as normal a life as possible. She finished high school with honors and friends, for the first time in her life, and went on to nursing school in Kansas City, getting as far away from Caroline as she could without jeopardizing her future. Caroline tortured her and her decisions over the phone, and now that she was working in St. Louis, the harassment had increased. But she let it go like water off a duck's back.

## A Newfound Sense of Freedom

Marissa Thomas rolled her eyes as she struggled with putting a bun in her hair while holding the cordless phone receiver to her ear with her shoulder. The sound of her mother's voice was much like a cheese grater scraping over her eardrum, and it was all she could do to remain respectful and pleasant.

"I hope you're eating enough," Caroline was saying sternly. "Being so sick, and sickly, your entire life is really nothing to play with, you know. Here you are, working crazy hours, and an outrageous amount of them, and you tell me you ate a peanut butter sandwich last night?"

Marissa popped the last needed bobby pin into her bun and sighed as she took the receiver into her hand and relieved her shoulder from the task of holding it. "Mother, I'm fine. If I'm hungry, I eat. If I'm thirsty, I drink. And if I'm tired, I sleep. You have nothing to worry about."

Her mom continued to fret into the phone, and Marissa listened with half of her attention only; the other half was busy looking for her left nurses' shoe. White with laces, a thick, slip-proof sole, and as ugly as they came. She limped around the room, one shoe on, searching for its twin while Caroline picked her nearly to death.

"You don't think I pushed through an entire lifetime of illness and hospitalization just for you to starve yourself, do you?" she was nagging. "And we both know that healthcare is the worst possible field. I mean, come on, Marissa. You have never been well yourself; how are you going to properly care for sick people when you're sickly yourself?"

Spotting the lost shoe beneath the far end of the sofa, Marissa hobbled over to it and plopped down to fetch it and put it on. She groaned into the phone and sat back hard on the couch, like a child preparing to have a fit. Marissa had been listening to garbage from her mother on one issue or another her entire life. And the talk of her being ill and sickly was just bullshit. Both of them knew why she had been so sick as a child and pre-teen, but Caroline talked about it like she had been the victim of some horrendous bug.

"Listen, Mother," she began, struggling to keep her voice steady and calm; disrespecting her mom was never, ever a good idea. "I promise you that I am taking care of myself, and you know how much I love my job. Why do you give me such grief over it? I just don't need to talk to you about this now."

"You know how I worry, and yet you belittle my love and concern by shooing me off when I try to talk to you like an adult," Caroline replied stiffly.

"Mother…"

"Done!" Caroline was almost growling now. "Just done!"

The phone went dead in Marissa's hand. She merely shook her head, smiled, and hung up the phone. Five or ten years ago she would have been trembling in her shoes at her mother's tone of voice. Now she was more than one-thousand miles away, and all the old woman could do was badger on and on. Yes, the bitching was still enough to make her tremble, but she was always saved by the hanging up that her mother did when Marissa didn't agree with her. Which was happening more and more the older she got, and that was enough to make Marissa very happy and satisfied.

She laid the phone on the coffee table and stood up and walked into the hallway, where she stood before the full-length mirror for a final look at herself. No makeup, hair in a bun, face scrubbed clean, and uniform flawless. Except for a single escaped wisp of hair at her temple, which she fixed with a spare bobby pin from her pocket, she looked the part she played: an innocent, dedicated, almost spinster-like nurse who worked on the pediatric unit at the Sisters of Compassion Health Care Center.

∞

Twenty minutes later she was sitting on the bus heading for work. Marissa always worked the three-to-eleven shift. It was the best, by far, because she was able to spend time with the children that the day nurses weren't able to spare. Once supper was done, she would play board games with the kids, watch movies, or just go from room to room and spend individual time talking with them, which they seemed to love. As the bus bounced down the busy street, she let her mind focus on her job and the kids on a deeper level.

Why had she chosen pediatrics? Her mother asked her this at least three times a week, and the truth was nothing like the answer she fed her mom. She would tell her mom that she loved the openness and honesty of children, and she loved being able to nurture the little ones. The truth was that she wanted to feel like their hero, and not a day went by that they didn't make her feel like exactly that. Sometimes it was for simple reasons, like picking out the right color bandage, or even kissing a boo-boo when other nurses or doctors weren't looking. She had only been nursing for just over a year. Some days she got to the really sick ones in time to give them another day of life, and nothing beat that. It had only happened twice, and it was true that there was a doctor present both times, but the children always gave her full credit, and she took it.

Her mind drifted then to the past. Oh, how many hospitals and doctors, and how many times she had tolerated, without confrontation or fight. There had been so much sickness and pain at the hand of her mother that all Marissa wanted to do was save any and every child who seemed to be suffering under the hand of neglect and complacency by the parents. Yes, she had been there when doctors saved children's lives in the past, and sure, she had been the one to bring the doctors to them in time to rescue them, but she had never really done the saving herself. This was what she aimed to do someday. She wanted everyone to know just how competent, caring, and professional she really was; the fact that the kids knew just wasn't enough for her.

∞

As of late, however, Marissa had been struggling with a single issue. The problem was her perspective on the parents of the children she nursed at work, both in the birthing center and on the adjoining pediatric ward. She felt that a majority of the parents were either careless with the children, negligent, or both, and she often found herself hovering over them or spying when they didn't think she was around. So far, no one had complained, though one other nurse who worked in the birthing center with her had told her to ease up a bit and let the parents be parents. The bottom line was that she honestly didn't feel that any of them could be trusted to do what was right for the children. This all tied into her upbringing and the way her mother had victimized her. Marissa now minimized what she had gone through with Caroline and didn't connect the past with her current behavior at all. In her mind, she was innocently doing her job, something they couldn't possibly understand.

# CHAPTER 7

Her stop was coming up next. She pulled the wire that rang the bell, embraced her belongings, and sat forward on the edge of her seat. As the bus pulled over to the curb and stopped, Marissa stood and paused at the open door to speak to the driver.

"Thanks, Jim. Hope you have a good route, and I'll see you in the morning?"

The man nodded and smiled. "Have a good shift, Marissa."

She stepped off the bus and crossed the parking lot, then went around to the side of the large building to the employee entrance. As she entered using her ID card and made her way down the hall to the elevator, co-workers in the break room greeted her and waved. She smiled in return but said nothing to encourage further conversation. After all, she didn't go to work to make friends; she went to make children well.

Today she was assigned to pediatrics rather than the birthing center. She got updates from the day nurse, went over the charts, and touched base with the two doctors who were still on the floor. Afterward, she dove into preparing her cart for her first rounds and med administrations, then set off down her assigned hall, humming as she went. Marissa went from room to room, greeting her small patients, listening to their stories, and giving them their meds. She made sure they were clean and on fresh linens. She took the time to collect urine samples that had been ordered for her shift. After an hour and a half, she reached her last room. Soon it would be time to pass out supper trays and deal with the patients with feeding tubes.

She entered the partially opened door of her last room. It housed a small four-year-old girl who had been struggling with a heart defect since birth. Her name was Amanda, and she had spent most of her short life in the hospital. It was nothing new to her at all, and she showed no fear at any procedure that needed to be done. Right now, she was hospitalized while she waited for a new heart. Marissa walked in with a smile.

"Hi, Amanda," she greeted with a smile as she got ready to take the girl's vitals. "How are you today?"

The child was exceptionally pale, more so than Marissa had ever seen her. "I'm tired. And I'm cold. I sure hope I get a new heart soon. My mommy had to go home because she couldn't stop crying. Daddy went down to the cafeteria to eat."

Marissa began the process of taking the girl's vitals while the child continued to tell her about the day in a voice that was just above a whisper. When she was finished, Marissa rolled the pole with her vital equipment away from the bed and sat down on the edge to tuck the child in better while the weak chatter continued.

Suddenly Amanda sucked in a deep breath, and her body arched as her eyes became glassy. The heart and respiration monitor began to go haywire, and Marissa sprang to action, pushing the button over the bed that called for a code blue. Sirens went off, and the words "Code Blue, Room 8b," began to shoot out of the hallway intercoms. Marissa was oblivious to the noise as she initiated CPR on the tiny girl on the bed.

She worked until she was pouring in sweat, speaking to the small child between the breaths she breathed into her body. "Stay with me, Amanda. We need you here… your mommy and daddy need you!" She continued to work vigorously and with great focus. After what seemed like an eternity, the tiny girl drew breath, her pulse and heartbeat returned and stabilized, and Marissa angrily wondered where her back-up was.

When she turned around, she saw them: two doctors and three nurses, all standing and smiling. The room was spinning, and she thought she might collapse. The small group just stared.

"Excellent job, Nurse Thomas," Dr. Hardy said as he faked clapping as to make no sound and disturb the patient. The other three nurses rushed to Amanda's bed to tend to her, while Dr. Hardy grabbed Marissa by the arm and led her gently into the hall.

"You saved that girl's life, you know," he said.
She looked at him, incredulous. "Dr. Hardy?"
"Yes?"
"I think I'm going to pass out," as she crumpled to

the floor.

∞

Marissa woke in one of the rooms used by the doctors and nurses who pulled double and triple shifts. At first, Marissa didn't know where she was, but when her mind and vision cleared, she saw many of her co-workers. They all gathered around and were grinning from ear to ear.

"The heroine awakes," Nurse Childers said, beaming.

Dr. Hardy nodded down at her. "Looks like we'll be buying the drinks tonight, dear."

Marissa sat up slowly. "How... how is Amanda?"

"She'll live to see another day, girl," Dr. Hardy said with a chuckle. "Thanks to you. How does it feel to single-handedly save the life of a child?"

Marissa thought about the question, then a smile spread over her face. "Like taking off in a rocket ship headed for outer space."

She had never felt so high in her life.

∞

The next week consisted of everlasting pats on the back, cakes and punch in the break room more than once, and articles about her in both the hospital newsletter and the St. Louis Times. The local news did a segment on her, and she was even lauded for saving the child in time for a new heart, which came three days later. Marissa Thomas was on top of the world.

# CHAPTER 8

But all good things come to an end.

A month later things were back to normal, and she began to feel betrayed, unappreciated and forgotten. As the ward got back to business as usual, her fame faded. Soon she began to feel lonely, ignored and angry. Most of all, she began to daydream about saving another child. However, each day passed with no incident, and her frustration grew.

It didn't take long for Marissa, with all of her life experience of sickness and her education of medicine, to begin to formulate a plan… a horrible, sick, selfish plot.

It began with reminiscing… well, stewing… over her mother and the past that Caroline had put her through. About six months prior, her mother had started trying to explain to her why she had done the things she did, how her father had abused and belittled her, and how she had felt the compelling need to prove herself at any cost. Marissa had listened half-heartedly before blowing up at the woman, telling her to shove her excuses. Then refused to discuss the issue further. Even though she had only half-listened, the half she had picked up was enough to spark recognition. What her mother had been describing to her was what she was feeling now: unappreciated, unrecognized, and under-valued. It was unbearable, and from the second she got home from work every night she cried herself to sleep. Upon waking, Marissa spent the day hours dreading going to work and hearing nothing in the way of complements or getting pats on the back. Each day she thought she could bear it a little less. But now she had an idea.

She could choose one of the children! Not one who was deathly ill, but one who was well enough to survive, yet adequately sick for some kind of attack or organ failure to be believed. She could efficiently administer a tiny amount of medication to the patient.

Something she could control… something that would allow her to maintain control and bring them back. That should do it; it should be enough to gain a bit more recognition. Just enough so she would feel wanted and needed again by her co-workers. Indeed, two saves would be sufficient in achieving the attention she deserved… and now so desperately craved.

Marissa opened the drawer on her nightstand and took out a spiral notebook and pen. She lay on her stomach on her bed, and by the light of the lamp on her nightstand began to plot the course she would take. She wrote down the names of every long-term patient on the pediatric ward, their diagnoses, and the treatments ordered for them by their attending physicians.

Then, Marissa began the slow, morbid process of

choosing just the right child to 'save.'

∞

A five-year-old boy who had been beaten severely by his stepfather, a drug addict and all-around bum. The boy hadn't focused on his plate of food one night at dinner. Instead, he had been distracted by a small television the man had playing in the dining room during a sporting event. This pissed the low-life off, and he had beaten the child within an inch of his life. When he was brought through the emergency room, he had a broken arm, dislocated shoulder, shattered cheekbone, and crushed foot, which the cockroach had stepped on over and over after the boy lost consciousness in an attempt to wake him up.

He went through surgery, then intensive care. After that, he was transferred to pediatrics for physical therapy and observation due to an ongoing issue with a punctured lung. While he seemed to be recovering on a timeline that was to be expected, every now and then he would go into a seizure and subsequently pass out. After much testing, doctors worked on medicating him for the seizures, but they just couldn't pinpoint the cause of the fainting. It was best to continue to test him and watch him until they had things figured out enough for him to leave.

Unfortunately, the mother only visited once a week. She had some strange idea that her husband wouldn't be in jail if the boy had just kept his eyes on his plate. He just needed to be a good boy for once! Each visit started well; the boy would be excited to see his mommy, and she seemed to feel the same upon seeing him. But before an hour was up, she would get so wound up and angry that the doctors had to ask her to leave. She would come back a week later, only to repeat the same thing all over again. It was atrocious. Finally, Marissa was directed by the boy's primary doctor to put an end to the visits altogether, which she did gladly. Children's Services was already involved. With the way the mother was behaving, it was surmised that the child would be placed in foster care.

He was a perfect specimen; he needed Marissa to take action fast.

With him, Marissa used an injection. She merely waited until naptime, and when he and his roommate were completely asleep, she would administer the cocktail. His breathing monitor began to sound almost all at once, at which point she ran into the boys' bathroom, flipped on the light, and then ran out just as another nurse was making an entrance. Of course, she got to him first, administering CPR, and got the child breathing again.

# CHAPTER 9

"Nurse Thomas, none of us sitting on this administrative board today is pleased with having to deal with the charges at hand, and I assure you that not one of us believes, at any level, that you are guilty of what you have been accused of doing."

Mr. Harrison James, the hospital administrator, was watching Marissa with both embarrassment and regret. Marissa sat stiffly in her chair facing the hospital board, consisting of Mr. James and the unit heads, all physicians. Behind her sat several other doctors and nurses, all in attendance for the sole purpose of giving her support. Also behind her sat the members of three different families, all related to children who Marissa had 'brought back' and revived. They also were her accusers, the ones who wanted her resignation, and they practically wanted it written in blood. As she clutched a shredded, damp tissue, she found herself wishing they were dead, but she took solace in the words of Mr. James. None of her co-workers, or he, believed that the charges against her held any merit whatsoever.

In the last two years, Marissa had saved six children, or approximately one every four months. She had received several citations, gained the highest respect of the hospital and its employees, and had even been promoted to head pediatric nurse four months prior. But two weeks ago, it had all started to crumble down around her.

It turned out that the parents of the last child she revived and the parents of another she had saved a few months earlier were very close, the best of friends, in fact. They met at a hospital sponsored support group for parents of children with terminal or chronic illness, and things had blossomed from there. When she saved the child of the latter parents, she had been celebrated as a hero, just as she was with the final one. Everything was going as planned.

Unbeknownst to her, the parents had all begun talking together, comparing notes, and drawing the parents of other little patients into their group to do the same. It didn't take long for them to convince each other that Nurse Marissa Thomas was playing a dangerous game with the children.

At first, they brought their suspicions to the hospital board, who basically shooed them away with all of Marissa's citations and newspaper articles. But they didn't give up so smoothly. Soon they threatened to involve police, if only for the sake of investigation if Marissa didn't resign her position. They didn't demand her license… they naturally wanted her gone from Sisters of Compassion, and they wanted her to leave the St. Louis area altogether.

"Do you have anything you would like to say, Nurse Thomas?"

The question came from the head of pediatrics, Dr. Miles Hardy, who had not only been her mentor but was one of her biggest supporters.

Marissa sniffed softly and dabbed at her eyes. "Isn't there any other way?"

All of the board members broke eye contact, some busying themselves by doodling on the notepads in front of them. After several seconds Mr. James met her eyes once again. They were filled with sadness and disgust.

"I'm afraid not. We have been threatened with loss of funding if action is not taken." Harrison James cleared his throat. "If you resign willingly, you will not only leave with relocation compensation, but you will also leave with the highest recommendation from those of us at this hospital." He shifted his gaze to the people seated behind her. "Fortunately, there is nothing anyone can do about that. But… if you do not tender your resignation willingly, we will be forced to terminate you without compensation or staff support. Do you know what you will choose, or do you need more time?"

Marissa just stared at him, then wiped her eyes one final time and took a deep breath. "Of course, I will resign. I have no desire to draw out this misery for all of you. I know the truth, as I believe all of you do: I would never harm a child. I am appreciative that you are willing to stand behind me as I enter a new phase in my life and career, and for that, I thank you from the bottom of my heart. Mr. James, you will have my resignation on your desk first thing in the morning."

# CHAPTER 10

Marissa sat in her gently-used new car and stared up at the seven-story, four-wing brick building before her. Southern State Community Hospital in Retribution, Texas operated on a smaller scale than what she was used to, but she saw that fact as a blessing. She could get to know her patients and their families on a deeper level and the town itself was small enough that she could all but disappear. Southern State had practically tripped over their own feet in its efforts to hire her, offering her a benefits package to die for, and even hiring her as the head nurse of pediatrics right off the bat. Her friends at Sisters of Compassion had been true to their word, protecting her from any chance of Southern State hearing any negative word about her, and they did a beautiful job of keeping her new location and place of employment under wraps.

But there was nothing to worry about because Marissa was done. She decided solidly that any recognition or attention she got, she would earn honestly. There would be absolutely no more risk-taking or putting children in harm's way. She was going to be the best nurse the small hospital had ever had, and she was going to knock their socks off.

Gathering her purse and other belongings, she got out of her car and locked it securely. She walked, head held high. With a broad smile on her face, she thought about her mother and how delightful it would have been for the woman to see her now, overcoming odds and coming out on top of the vultures. Caroline Thomas would see no such thing. She had died of a heart attack six weeks earlier, unable to deal with the fact that her daughter had been accused of harming children and then resuscitating them for the sake of attention. In the end, she wouldn't even speak to her daughter on the phone, and then one day Marissa got the call from one of her mother's neighbors in Florida... she had passed quietly in the night.

Marissa couldn't have cared less. After all, the nagging and bitching would have only been a detriment to her plans to do things properly. When her mother was in her life and in her ear, she frequently ended up hating herself, and that was always when she chose another child to save. Her mother being gone was the most liberating, satisfying thing that had happened to her in her entire life. She planned to embrace her newfound sense of freedom.

She entered through the employee door, showed her crisp, new plastic photo badge to the security guard, and flashed him a big smile. She had met him on the day of her initial interview; his name was Raymond Smith, and she guessed him to be around her age. He had dark hair and brown eyes that managed to exude softness, even though they were planted in the skull of one who had to be tough if required.

"Nurse Thomas! Welcome!" He flashed her a return grin that showed off perfect white teeth. "I can tell you, we are sure proud to have someone with your skill and talent join the team here at Southern State. Do you remember how to get to pediatrics? If not, I would be happy to escort you."

Marissa was more than tempted; after all, she hadn't been on a date since she snuck out her bedroom window in high school to hang out at a keg party in the woods. That little jaunt had earned her a beating that had almost pulverized her face, and her mother had to call her in sick for a week to school. She was also locked in her room, with the window nailed shut, and only given drink mix and crackers for sustenance.

"I would love that, but I do remember. It's probably best for me to get used to the hospital's layout on my own anyway." She offered him another smile and a quick wink. "Thanks, Mr. Smith."

"Call me Raymond, please."

With an almost flirty nod, Marissa made her way up the long hall to the staff lounge, where she was to clock into her shift before reporting to pediatrics for a morning meeting with Dr. Clifford Helmsworth, head of the department. She had opted for the morning shift this time around because of the head nurse position. The truth was, her primary tasks, besides supervising her staff, would consist of much charting, meetings with doctors, and computer work. She was going to have to really manipulate her schedule if she was to get to know the children at all or spend any kind of quality time with them. She would figure it out, no matter what. The children were the primary reason she became a nurse in the first place.

Within fifteen minutes Marissa was seated comfortably in a large leather armchair in an office that was surprisingly large for the size of the hospital which housed it. Dr. Helmsworth, had worked in private practice for the first ten years of his career before joining the health crew at Southern State and taking root. The large, almost clumsy looking man with silver hair moved and spoke with unexpected grace and charm. Marissa guessed that the children loved him.

"I want to welcome you, once again, to our team, Marissa," he said with a fatherly smile. "You come highly recommended, and I can imagine that Dr. Hardy up in St. Louis was extremely disappointed to see you go. Tell me again, why you opted to leave the Sisters of Compassion and come to Retribution?"

Marissa took a sip of the coffee his secretary had provided her with when she arrived, then smiled shyly at the doctor. "I just felt the need for something… smaller. I want to be able to connect with the children on a quality level, a level that I wasn't able to reach working in a facility the size of Sisters." She paused, then held up her hand slightly. "Don't misunderstand, please. I realize that as head nurse on the unit I will primarily be pushing a pencil and reporting the results, but it is my full intention to do whatever it takes to make sure my patients, small as they may be, know me and trust me… my staff as well. If that means spending my off time here, then that is what you will see me do." With a smile and a light chuckle, Marissa added, "What I do is my life, Doctor. It is what I wake up for."

The man beamed. "Well, my dear, we're sold. I can't wait to turn the unit over to you and see what you can do. Now, for the next week, you will be spending much time with myself and each of the other doctors who have hospital privileges. There are only two who are permanent employees here for the peds unit: myself and Dr. Stein; you'll meet him later on today. You will also be shown the ropes by the nurses on the unit. I expect you plan to hold a nursing meeting with your staff right away?"

"As a matter of fact, sir, I have an itinerary made up… as vague as it may be at present, that will give all of us a solid guideline for showing me hospital procedure and then allowing me to make any changes I believe are needed for improvement. I am sure, however, that these changes will be small. The unit is probably as efficient as it can get."

That was when the man's smile faded. He sat back in his desk chair and crossed his arms over his chest. "Unfortunately, you are a bit off on your assessment in that area. While I cannot go into details, the fact of the matter is that the last department nursing head we had simply didn't have the necessary grip on organization required in a medical facility, and she had even less of a hold on her staff. Needless to say, numerous issues could have been life threatening for one of our patients. For example; this is something that was in the papers, so I feel completely comfortable divulging it to you, the woman had so little control that she had nurses and doctors engaging in sexual activity during rounds, stealing patient medications, and the like. It was a huge mess and one that we are still cleaning up. This is why we brought you in."

Marissa first shook her head at his revelation, then smiled and nodded at his last statement.

"You are aware that you will be short two RNs for the time being?" He asked.

She quickly processed his words and replied, "I was not. Until the gap is filled, I am more than willing to pick up the slack. I have absolutely no problem choosing a quality nurse or two to do it with me."

Helmsworth grinned, showing off perfect, though slightly yellowing, teeth, and said, "I knew you'd say that... I just knew it. Now, Nurse Thomas, let's go meet your team."

# CHAPTER 11

Marissa opened her eyes to the sun shining on her face and the tantalizing aroma of hot coffee dancing in her nose. She smiled and stretched a long, leisurely stretch… the kind one only sees on television commercials and movies. With a great big yawn, she swung her feet over the side of the bed and into her slippers. She was naked, so the fact that she put her slippers on at all struck a chord of comedy in her brain, and she smiled lazily.

Making her way over to the bathroom door, Marissa grabbed her robe off the hook inside. She wrapped it around herself, then padded out to the living room, making not a sound. There he was, Raymond Smith, still naked himself, pouring coffee and singing to the radio. She watched him, smiling as he cut loose with no self-consciousness or hesitation.

Raymond took a long sip of his coffee before breaking into a chorus with the music playing on the classics station.

Marissa couldn't resist cutting in at the top of her lungs. "Because you're all I need!"

Raymond immediately put his coffee down and

turned to her, his face ten shades of red. "How long have you been standing there?" He asked as he turned down the radio's volume.

"Forever," she giggled.

He turned his back to her, but she could tell by the sound of his voice that he was now smiling. "Well, you're one to poke fun. You should see your hairdo."

She ran absent-minded fingers through her sandy mane and laughed. "Is that all you've got? I just woke up. Cheap shot."

She walked over to him and wrapped her arms around him from behind, so she could plant kisses on his back and shoulders. "Good morning," she moaned.

"Good morning to you." Raymond turned around to face her, one arm keeping her pressed against his body, the other holding a steamy cup of coffee in her favorite mug. "I was just getting ready to bring this to you, lady."

"Mmm, thank you." She took the mug, planted a quick kiss on his cheek, and leaned back against the counter to sip the required hot liquid. After a few drinks, she smiled at him. "Are you planning to get dressed today?"

Raymond shrugged as he wiped down the countertop. "I don't know for sure. It is one of the only days off we've had together in two months. No, I think not. I believe I should remain in the raw, just in case, for the duration of the day."

Reaching out, Raymond grabbed the sash of her robe and gave it a gentle tug. Her wrap fell open, revealing Marissa's nakedness. She didn't even flinch, only offered him a smile with her eyes over the rim of her coffee cup. When she took it away from her mouth, he gently retrieved it from her hand and set it on the counter, forgotten. In seconds she was in his arms, and they were kissing passionately, and only moments later the two of them were on the kitchen floor, her fluffy robe protecting their naked bodies from the cold tile as they slowly made love.

∞

Afterward, they both lay there staring at the ceiling, her robe pulled awkwardly over their shoulders, their bodies glistening in sweat. "I'm glad we got this place, you know?" Marissa was speaking in a dreamy voice. "It's perfect, with all the extra room. We could be here for a long time, even if we decide to have babies."

"That's why we got it, right?" Raymond nuzzled her shoulder with his nose. "The wedding is just around the corner. Babies will come soon enough."

"I can hardly wait," she replied softly.

The two of them spent the rest of the day in their love nest, lazing in front of the television, snacking, and dozing off now and then. They made love two more times that day before falling asleep at twilight, with a monster movie on the set, and nestled in each other's arms. Right before dozing off, Marissa was thankful for the way her life was going, and she smiled at herself for overcoming the evil she had fallen into while at Sisters of Compassion. That evil had been the only real legacy her mother had left for her, and she had beaten it down and won. Now she had a life, an incredible career, and she was going to marry the perfect man in only five short months. The woman who gave her birth would turn over in her grave if she knew how happy the daughter she had continually tried to kill had come to be.

She was winning.

# CHAPTER 12

Marissa jotted down some numbers on the sheet fastened to her clipboard. Inventory was one of the worst parts of her job, but only because the small storeroom was so hot and stuffy. She wiped the back of her hand across her forehead, scribbled her signature at the bottom of the requisition sheet, and sighed with relief as she reached for the doorknob. Finally, she was done with this task for another week.

She made her way to her office, to enter the figures into the computer before turning over the paperwork to the head of the receiving and delivery department. But just as she reached for the knob of her door, she was startled by the voice of one of her nurses behind her.

"Marissa! We need you in room 425! Stat!" It was Mary Calvert, one of her best nurses, and if she were honest, the closest person in her life to a friend that she had, besides Raymond.

She didn't miss a beat. Without thought, she placed the clipboard in the file holder attached to her office door beneath her name tag and bolted off behind Mary toward room 425. Mary entered the room a full five seconds before her, and just as she reached the door she thought to herself how odd it was to not hear any calls over the intercom for the emergency, but the thought was fleeting.

She swung the door open, catching it before it closed entirely behind her anxious co-worker, and entered, ready for action.

"Congratulations, Marissa!"

The room was full of pediatric staff, including Dr. Helmsworth and his secretary. Balloons were floating around, streamers dangling from the ceiling, and a banner with the same words they had just shouted written in large, bright pink letters across it. She was immediately embarrassed and taken aback by the gesture, which motivated her to look back out the door to see if any other staff were in on the deal but running late. All she saw was a scattering of tiny patients' faces peeking out of their doors and smiling brightly.

"Oh, you guys!" She shook her head and fought back the tears.

The day before, during final rounds before her shift's end, Marissa had been called to Dr. Helmsworth's office. This always made her tense up; even if they had not been aware of the accusations against her at Sisters of Compassion, she carried them around daily. It wasn't altogether impossible that the truth could reach her new place of employment. Every time the doctor called for her she got a sense of panic and fear, and yesterday had been no exception.

Instead, he had offered her the opportunity to not only head the pediatrics nursing department, but also that of the labor and delivery unit on the opposite wing. Yes, it would double her workload, but it would give her some invaluable experience in the field of neonatal and birth and infant care while adding fifteen-thousand dollars to her paycheck every year. She was not only excited, but she was also beside herself and jumped at the opportunity. It was a promotion that she never saw coming. Now she had the chance to spread herself out to every child in the facility, and she could barely contain her glee.

"Well," Mary said as she poured sparkling grape juice into a cup and handed it to Marissa, "you deserve a lot more recognition than just a couple of 'way to go's' in the hall in passing."

"I'd have to agree," she replied, her cheeks blushing. "Thank you all. You don't know what this means to me."

Dr. Helmsworth lifted his sparkling juice and smiled. "Here's to Nurse Marissa Thomas, who has changed the pediatric unit for the better, by a far cry. May she do the same with L & D and may her future shine as brightly as her beautiful smile!"

"Hear, hear!!"

Everyone drank, and for the next ten minutes the group of workers laughed and patted her on the back. It was all the time they could take from the children and the unit responsibilities. Marissa was in a daze, for she had never imagined what her life would be like today, especially when she was seated before the board at Sisters of Compassion being dismissed by the very people she thought were her friends. She felt a twinge of anger at the parents who had led the bandwagon of her demise there but quickly dismissed it. Let them eat cake, she thought.

As they wrapped things up, Mary and two other nurses pulled her aside and told her they planned to take her for dinner and drinks after their shift. Mary told her to run home as soon as she got off, get changed, and meet them all at Margarita's Mexican Cafe in nearby San Antonio. She agreed and left the room for her office to finish up the supply order and call Raymond. She had to tell him of her plans. Marissa knew he wouldn't mind; they had made their own plans to celebrate her promotion that weekend by having a Sunday brunch together and playing miniature golf at Rudy's Mini Putt.

Three o'clock came quickly, with all she had to do, but she didn't get out the door until nearly four-thirty. She let Mary know she was running late with a quick phone call, then spent just over a half-hour saying goodbye to 'her' kids and making sure the next shift was up to date on each little soul. It only took her twenty minutes at home to get changed and apply some simple makeup, and before she knew it, Marissa was in San Antonio with the girls, enjoying every single second of their love and attention. It seemed she couldn't soak it up enough.

"So," a nurse named Tanya Radcliff asked after dinner, while they enjoyed their second jumbo margaritas, "how proud is Mr. Raymond Smith, hmm? How does the best security guard in the world feel about his soon-to-be wife climbing the ranks as she is?"

Marissa shrugged and blushed. "He's happy. You know, this is coming at such a good time. Now we'll be able to really have a nice wedding next month, and hopefully, in a couple of years, we can start a family. He was actually ecstatic. I was surprised."

Talk of Raymond suddenly caused a pull at her brain. It had been strange that he hadn't been home when she went there to change. She had told him she would be there, and he had even mentioned that he would see her then. Marissa had been in such a hurry due to her lateness that she hadn't given his absence more than a passing thought.

Mary diverted her attention. "Well, don't get started on babies too soon; we have plenty here who need you, and so do we."

With that, Marissa steered the conversation toward other things. She discussed the labor and delivery unit and asked the women for their feedback on what they liked or disliked about the way things had been running there. They gossiped about the old head nurse, telling vulgar stories of promiscuous behavior on the unit and blatant drug use. Marissa had worked the floor on two occasions, but it had seemed to be fine from her perspective. Of course, the regular nurses and their head nurse would have particularly minded their behavior with her around. They would have assumed she would be appalled at their reindeer games, and they would have been right.

"So, when do you start?" Jenny asked.

Marissa took a sip of her drink, sighed, and sat back. "Let's see… Monday I'm coming in early to work peds and take care of any needs there, plus I'll want to look in on the kids. You know, the normal stuff. Helmsworth told me he trusted me to work out how I want to split up my time, so I think after lunch I'll head over to L & D and spend the rest of the afternoon. I plan to shadow nurses, meet any new parents, and basically watch how they are doing things for the first week or two. That includes everything, by the way, not just how they handle patient care. I want to go over inventory, cover their medication orders and make sure they match up to what's on hand, and I want to talk to each nurse individually to get their perspective on what had been going on and what they would like to see changed. I figure I'll be pulling twelve to fifteen-hour days for who knows how long. But I'm fine with it; it's the nature of the beast."

She got nods of agreement and groans from all around, then Tanya held up her massive margarita glass. "Here's to all the nurses who dedicate their lives to making things better. What would the world do without them?"

Glasses clinked and were drained, and after ordering one more apiece, they sat and chatted loosely about each other's lives. They discussed their men and their children if they had any. Mary told a couple of hilarious stories from her days in nursing school, and Marissa thoroughly enjoyed every moment.

At 7:30, her cell phone chimed after the toast, and

her eyes lit up when she saw it was Raymond. "How late were you going to be out, babe?" he asked. "I thought I might head over to Josh's and check out his new man cave... he says his pool table came today."

Marissa glanced at each of the girls. "How late do you think we'll be? It's Raymond, and he wants to know if he has time to visit a friend."

Mary laughed hard. "10:30, at least! Tell him not to worry; if you get too wasted, Jen can drive your car and follow us while I take you home."

She gave the information to her man, exchanged 'I love you's, and hung up. Marissa had never felt so good, though she attributed most of it to her buzz. With gusto, she picked up where she left off with the girls, and time continued to pass. By the time they were ready to leave it was only 8:45, and even though she thought it should have been much later, Marissa was more than willing to get home. Having never been too much of a drinker, the tequila was going straight to her head and realizing she had overdone it a bit, Marissa took Mary up on her offer of a ride.

While Jen followed them in Marissa's car, Mary steered toward the home Marissa shared with Raymond. The woman listened to Marissa go on and on excitedly about her fiancé, slurring her words as she chattered about his attributes and how lucky she was to have found him. She talked about the promotion and how excited she was, then went into her nervousness at heading the nurses on two units at the same time. Before she knew it, Mary was pulling up to the curb in front of her house, and Jen was pulling the car into the driveway.

"Looks like Raymond wasn't out as late as he thought," Mary observed. "His car's in a spot, and one of the lights is on."

Marissa looked at the house through the darkness with one eye closed for focus, saw the light, and recognized that it was coming from their bedroom. "He must have taken all their money playing pool and wore himself out." She broke into laughter, said goodbye to her friend, and stumbled a bit as she got out of the vehicle. "Good thing I wore flats," she said to Mary with a smile.

After Jen was buckled into Mary's car, the two pulled away, and Marissa started across the yard to the main walk, weaving slightly and humming a song she had heard at the restaurant. Making it up the small flight of stairs to their front door, she tried the knob on the door, but it was locked. Fortunately, the porch light made finding her key easily enough; it was just a matter of closing one eye again, as was fitting it into the keyhole.

Inside she was confronted with mostly darkness, except for the light over the stove in the kitchen. She could hear the television playing softly from the bedroom, and a handful of steps heading up allowed her to see the light coming from beneath the bedroom door. Marissa smiled. How sweet, she thought. He's waiting for me, probably naked.

Trying her best to be quiet walking up the stairs, she

removed her jacket and slipped off her shoes, then tossed her purse onto the accent table next to her. She strolled through the dimly lit hall toward the bedroom, unzipping the skirt she was wearing as she went and letting it drop to the floor. In nothing but panties and a black satin crop top, she took hold of the doorknob and opened the bedroom door.

"Honey, I'm home," she greeted with a smile.

Raymond and a blond woman who looked incredibly like the main hospital receptionist both turned their heads toward her in surprise. Marissa's smile slowly faded as she processed what she was seeing: Her fiancé and another woman, were staring at her from her own bed, his ass bared for all to see. She literally felt her heartbreak in her chest.

"Mar-Marissa? What are you doing here?"

She snorted slightly, fighting tears which she refused to let come.

"I live here," she replied softly.

The girl beneath him began to squirm her way out from under him, jumped off the bed, and grabbed her garments from the floor. "I… I'm sorry. I should go."

Marissa stepped aside and held the door open as the woman scrambled past her, pulling her jeans on as she went. Raymond was digging around under the blankets, probably for his underwear. Marissa held her position, keeping the door open and staring at him through eyes that were seeing the truth. She wanted to vomit all over him.

"Honey, I'm sorry. I didn't…"

Marissa chuckled and shook her head. "Just get out, will you."

Her voice was still, forceful, and threatening. Raymond looked at her in disbelief as he pulled his boxer briefs on. "Can't we talk about this?"

"Absolutely not." Her voice was hardly more than a whisper.

Raymond was now putting on his khaki cargo shorts. "I could sleep in the spare room… we can talk in the morning."

"You can sleep on her couch, for all I care, but you aren't staying here." She looked him directly in the eyes, suddenly so sober that closing one of them was no longer needed. "The house is in my name, remember? You can leave. Don't worry; I won't set fire to your things. You can come to get them all in a couple of days. But just go."

With that, Marissa closed the bedroom door softly and flipped the hall light on, so she could find her skirt. Once it was on, she sat in the barely-lit living room staring straight ahead and thinking no thoughts whatsoever. She was in shock, and she felt like it was all a dream. As she sat there, she tried to wake up. She was never touching another drop of booze as long as she lived.

Raymond grabbed a few items and shoved them into his gym bag. While he was scrambling to get the necessities, he heard Marissa say in a loud, monotone voice, "Please take the bedding off and take it with you." With a groan, he balled the sheets and pillowcases up, tied the outer layer in a knot, and headed out of the room and down the steps with his bag and the bedding in hand.

"Marissa, I..."

She continued to stare straight ahead, and with no emotion stated, "I know, I know. You feel terrible; you never meant for it to happen, it just happened. It will never happen again. You love me; you're so sorry. You're a horrible human being, and how can you make it up to me. Well, let me answer all those things with a simple fuck off. Now leave."

Raymond stood there, hands full and face flushed, just staring at her, waiting and hoping that she would suddenly change her mind. He was kicking himself, but the truth was, he wasn't doing it very hard. Yes, as he stood there waiting in the uncomfortable silence and dim light, he felt terrible, but there was no real remorse. Mostly he regretted being caught because he had fallen into a good thing with Marissa.

After what seemed like hours but was only a minute, Raymond walked to the front door, opened it, and paused. "I hope you call me. I hope you can forgive me."

Marissa didn't even flinch, and he knew it was time to go. So, without another thought, Raymond went, closing the door quietly behind him. The first thing he did when he pulled his car out and got on the road was dial Sheila, the hospital receptionist's number. It wouldn't do to spend money on a hotel room. He was going to have to pinch pennies without Marissa to have his back.

The soft sound of the door closing behind her didn't even faze Marissa. Already she had wiped Raymond out of her mind; that was the best way, after all. There was no sense in hanging on to it, and there would be no second chances. He couldn't be trusted to be faithful, which meant he couldn't be trusted with anything. Raymond was out, and good riddance to bad rubbish.

As if she were a robot, Marissa rose from her chair with jerky motions and went to the hall closet. There, she chose a clean set of linen and pillowcases and proceeded to make the bed. Afterward, just as she had every night of her life, with or without Raymond, she changed into shorts and a white tank top undershirt, brushed her teeth, and crawled into bed. She was sound asleep in no time, and she hadn't even shed a single tear.

# CHAPTER 13

The following Monday Marissa began the task of getting to know the nurses and procedures on her new unit. In the morning, she did her rounds on the pediatric ward, checked charts, and assured her team that things would smooth out and feel more ordinary with the passage of time. The afternoon she dedicated to labor and delivery, thinking things over, and making notes of changes that needed to be made. She figured it would take a couple of weeks of splitting up her days before she would be able to relax and split the two units up by days instead.

She let work consume her because when she worked, she didn't think about the pain of betrayal. On no occasion did she mention to any of her friends at work, particularly Mary and the others she had been out with, what happened when she got into her house that night. Instead of her usual friendly self, she was stiff and business-like, even with Mary, and she considered them to be reasonably close. On a couple of occasions during that first couple of weeks following Raymond's infidelity, Mary tried to start conversations meant to get Marissa talking, because she was beginning to worry.

The head nurse just wasn't herself. There were constant undertones that felt bad to Mary in everything about Marissa, her personality, and the way she did her job. But both times she tried, Marissa offered a stiff smile and thanked her not to pressure her into talking when she didn't want to. It didn't take long for the two women to become distant, and that was how Marissa wanted it.

Little did she, or anyone else know, that something had snapped inside of her mind.

It may have been apparent in her affect, but it sure didn't show in her work. If anything, her all-business disposition caused her to do a more impressive job than ever. She was quickly whipping the labor and delivery unit into shape, and the peds unit was running like a finely-tuned machine. None of it meant anything; once again, she felt like she was fading into the nothingness of life, that she was nothing special, and what she did do received no recognition. Those she considered friends had stopped being personal and even avoided her. She blamed them entirely, utterly oblivious to her own self-induced distance from them. She knew it was their doing because in her mind she was still Marissa. Her mother had always been right: People would turn from you for any reason, and they would fade away to suit their own needs.

Sure, Mary had tried to talk to her, and sure she had resisted. But if Mary had really cared, had truthfully been her friend, she would have pulled it out of her, nagged her into spilling her guts. But she didn't.

The tickle in her mind started three months after she rid herself of Raymond completely. Thoughts of taking control of the opinions of those around her and reminding them how indispensable she really is was starting to flirt with her. As she did her daily duties impeccably, she pushed them away, sometimes having to put up a fight that caused her to seek refuge in an empty room to gather her thoughts. She didn't fight the temptation to harm a child and bring it back because it was wrong; she fought the reverie because the child had to be the right child, with the right parents and the right circumstances. So, she struggled against the compulsion over and over again.

That was until a six-year-old was brought through emergency by ambulance with a severe nosebleed that could not be stopped. The mother reported to ER workers that it hadn't happened before, but she couldn't be sure. The woman's brains were mush… it was unmistakable she was on drugs of some kind.

The child, a little girl named Tara, told doctors and nurses that she had bloody noses all the time. Most of the time her mommy could stop them, but it took a long time. She was always tired, and she couldn't keep her food down. The nosebleed was contained, and the child was admitted to pediatrics for testing. Within three days doctors diagnosed her with leukemia. The worthless mother was told over the phone. She hadn't visited little Tara once so far.

Now the thoughts did more than tug at Marissa's

brain. After each short visit with Tara, they began to scream and make demands. It didn't take long for Marissa to give in. Not only would it put a good scare into that worthless mother but stopping the girl's heart and bringing her back would also get her some of the recognition that had so quickly faded. It wouldn't hurt the child a bit because she would be there; it would all be over in a matter of mere moments.

So, on day five of Tara's stay, while she was beginning to nap after tossing up her lunch while her three-year-old roommate slept soundly, Marissa did her rounds, and while in Tara's room she injected a wee bit of medication into the child's IV. Soon she was setting off a code blue and enjoying the rush of fighting to bring back a life through CPR. Surrounded by co-workers and a doctor tossing out orders, she worked herself into a sweat. Just like the pro that she was, the girl's heart began to beat again.

Then it was like old times. Pats on the back, stokes on her ego, and abundant thanks from a mother who suddenly saw fit to pull herself together. Marissa was finally in heaven once again, and she wondered why she ever stopped. Forgotten was the forced resignation at Sisters of Compassion. Gone was the memory of the fear of being caught and going to prison. All was right with the world and the thing she had done to Tara had brought all the wrong to a new-found glory.

She was going to start paying very close attention; there were many more children who really needed her.

Halloween approached quickly and the kudos began to dwindle once again.

At first, Marissa was tempted to panic that reality was setting back in. Then she began to get angry. Finally, she decided to get her emotions under control and start looking for another needy patient. As soon as she pulled herself and her thoughts together, she felt better.

That particular mental process took place at about 3:30 in the morning as she lay wide awake in her bed waiting for her alarm to go off. By the time it rang at 5:30 she was already showered, dressed, and humming to herself. It was a brand-new day, and the solution to her problems was right in the palm of her hand, so to speak. She could hardly wait to get to work.

Her goal for the day was simple: find a child who 'needed' her. If it didn't happen today, it would happen soon, because she was going to peel her eyes and her heart to the situation. The only thing her mother ever gave her was this gift, and the excuse for a woman had done it inadvertently. But nonetheless, she gave her the ability to spot one in need and help them, and through the situation pull herself and her life out of whatever rut it was in.

Sure, Caroline had only had one 'needy' child: her. What had she needed? In her mother's eyes, a father. What situation did her mother use her and her 'sicknesses' to pull herself out of? Lack of personal validation and the need for a man. Did she really succeed? Absolutely not. The woman died alone.

But Marissa was better than that, better than her. She had to agree that Mommy Dearest's theories were spot on, but her technique was practically non-existent. The woman never thought outside the box. How could one use their own child to have their needs met? Well, she would not only get her personal needs met, but she would also see to it that whatever the child was lacking would manifest through her actions as well.

So many events, so much trauma. That was what led to the beginning of a long chain of systematic abuse carried out by twenty-four-year-old Marissa Thomas. It stemmed from a mindset of self-preservation and brokenness dressed as an act of mercy each and every time. Each subtle attack on the tiny patients of that hospital would hail her a hero... temporarily, but each would also be a vital part of a means to an end to a reign of terror carried out by a woman living in a deep delusional fantasy. A fantasy in which she was the center of the universe.

# CHAPTER 14

Nurse Marissa Thomas became known as the savior of both children and newborn babies at Southern State Health Center, and all of it was orchestrated by her hand.

In her sublime stream of evilness, she 'saved' a total of six infants and kids during that period. While that may not seem like a lot by big-city standards, in a town the size of Retribution she was a walking miracle. And she was as good at planning and causing the near-deaths as she was at resuscitating the patients she was killing, be it ever so temporarily. She had it down to such a fine art that she never feared that she couldn't carry it out, never apprehensive of her plan failing, and it never did.

The rush she got each and every time became weaker with each attack. The feeling of satisfaction, superior intelligence, and adoration grew more and more short-lived. Marissa began to consider going through with the worst, actually letting one die. Perhaps if that happened, and she demonstrated to everyone how broken it would make her, she would feel right again.

She had nearly lost her mind completely.

But she would never let herself cross that line. Yes, she thought on it, fantasized about it, even went so far as to choose specific children to fantasize about. But she was not entirely convinced that what she would be doing was right, though she was convinced that what she was already doing was okay.

∞

It was a great feeling, and the attention lasted several weeks, making her wonder why she had waited so long to act. But, the recognition wasn't as intense, and it seemed to begin to wane much sooner than before.

This left her frustrated, bitter, and even more stoic than before.

Being a highly intelligent woman, she knew it was unfeasible to act too soon and find another child. Besides, the chance of another perfect kid showing up on one of her two units so quickly was slim to none. She would have to bide her time and find a way to get by. But the fact was that there was no other way to get by. Marissa knew as sure as she knew her own name that she was going to be miserable... emotionally dead, until the next opportunity came. It would be easy to jump the gun and just do it, but that kind of impatience would be her demise. She sat there on her bed in her home pondering all of these things, and then all the anger and frustration overcame her. She buried her face in the pillow, let the tears fall, and screamed into the pillow's thick stuffing so no one would hear. While she sobbed, she hit the mattress with her left fist, over and over, visualizing that the bed was first her mother, then

Raymond, and finally herself. Her thrashing and pounding and sobbing lasted only a brief moment, perhaps thirty seconds. Her body went limp, and she gave a few more whimpers before dozing off in her awkward position.

∞

Marissa had about reached her limit. She was edgy, moody, and rarely socialized with her co-workers, even on the most basic level. Mary, Jen, and Dr. Helmsworth himself took her aside, one by one, on more than one occasion, to inquire what was wrong and how they could help. Of course, they were all aware of the breakup with Raymond, but they tactfully left the topic out of all conversations. But they did make sure to show their concern to the point that it annoyed her. Fortunately, that's what friends are for anyway, right? While a part of her appreciated their courtesy, the other part, the part that tortured her mind and kept her up at night, that part was disgusted by them and their unwillingness to reach out and make her spill her guts. She blamed them, as she had come to blame everyone in her life for her troubles, past, present, and future. They were just a part of her professional life that she had to tolerate, and so she did just that as best as she could.

By the time little Lori came she was more than ready. At the first spark of realization that the child would be a perfect tool in her bizarre plan she began to devise her scheme. Usually, she would have invested a lot of time putting what she was going to do together, but Marissa felt an urgency that couldn't be resisted. It was the best option anyway, considering that the child had a mild heart condition. This was the reason for her admittance; exhaustion and inability to keep up with other kids her age at school had caused much concern, so she was there for a few days to undergo tests and monitoring in hopes of figuring it all out.

Lori lived with her dad; her mother was deceased. The man worked long, hard hours in construction, mostly in San Antonio, which called for a commute as well. He was struggling with all of that plus the responsibility of caring for his daughter alone.

Marissa assisted him with all that with a single injection of the solution into the girl's saline IV one evening during shift change. Fortunately, she roomed alone, and by innocently pretending to spend time with the kids like she usually did Marissa was able to carry out the deed. She was even able to slip out of Lori's room before the heart monitor went off and step into the med closet. She finally heard the monitor, which seemed to take forever. Marissa merely stepped from the closet, a stricken look on her face, and ran in with the other three nurses who were running that direction.

Marissa knew that the very sight of her, her very presence, caused the other nurses to step back and allow her to take the reins. Once again, she did just that, and by the end of the day, she was once more the celebrated health care worker with a knack for saving lives and being on her toes. This time, however, while she soaked up the worship and basked in the glory of her peers, she didn't let it show. For the first time, Marissa refused to let her own elation show. She acted tired, humble, and made a strong point of letting everyone know how much she despised the fact that life-saving measures were ever even needed. This garnered her even more attention, and she realized that the more she shrank back, the more they seemed to adore her.

The child's father was no exception. He was not only thankful, but he also came down with a sudden case of nurse love. He was smitten! While rugged and good-looking, Marissa wasn't interested, and she stiffly refused him several times, hurting his feelings and loving it.

∞

Time brought a new child into her path, and once again she went through the same old routine. The results were just as successful, but for the first time, she felt a twinge of boredom with her method. But it was safe and she was careful with her choice of patients. Marissa decided to begin to consider other ways to accomplish the same goal.

She was escalating, and to such a degree that one of her co-workers was becoming a tiny bit wary. Mary Calvert, who had been relatively close to Marissa in the past, had begun having an odd feeling with each occurrence involving a child patient nearly dying and being resuscitated. It wasn't that she thought the worst, or even suspected her one-time friend and confidante on a direct level. She just felt that the circumstances each time were a bit off kilter. She couldn't seem to put her finger on what she thought was going on; she knew Marissa better than anyone else, including her ex-fiancé. In her mind, there was simply no way Marissa would harm a child. She just thought the circumstances were odd, so much so that she often thought about each one over and over, trying to pinpoint the source of her concern.

Indeed, it was odd that there had been so many code blues. That probably wouldn't raise suspicion in a big city hospital, but in one the size of Southern State it was atrocious if she was honest with herself. Even if there was nothing fishy going on, so many attacks could be due to nothing short of negligence, at the very least.

So, if it wasn't Marissa, who was it that was causing the problems? Was anyone even doing it at all? They were questions that would not be answered for Mary Calvert right away, so she intermittently pondered and ignored the issue, even almost convincing herself that it was all in her head.

# CHAPTER 15

The next patients that came to face their near-death experiences were pretty much run-of-the-mill, and Marissa found herself bored and dissatisfied like never before. It was time to take things to another level and she planned to use another nurse, unbeknownst to her, to get the job done and take all the credit. It would be interesting to see someone reveling in grief over something they blamed themselves for entirely while Marissa soaked up the attention from the act of humility and false concern that she would show others.

By this point, Mary had her antennae. Months ago, she would have given her life to prove that Marissa would never harm another, she now thought she had assessed the situation horribly. But then something happened that switched her thinking one more time. Something happened that indicated the culprit was another person entirely.

∞

A seven-year-old girl was admitted to pediatrics with an initial diagnosis of Type I juvenile diabetes. She was checked in for stabilization and to train her family on her condition and the at-home use of insulin.

Unfortunately, what should have been an ordinary case that gave the child several quality years of life turned out to be a nightmare for the family that they wouldn't soon forget.

After the child's first night at Southern State, Marissa spent half the night at home, wide awake in her bed, thinking how she would do it. She had chosen the kid as soon as she got the file from the admissions office and it excited her. She had been waiting for a diabetic opportunity and now one had fallen right into her lap. She took notes, obsessed, and made it the center of her thought; every waking moment was spent daydreaming about the deed. Finally, on the patient's third day in, she decided to act.

She was most excited about the execution of her plan this time around. Marissa didn't intend to be in the room at all; she would assist in the preparation of the medication cart as usual for the LPN to administer afternoon dosages as she always did. But she tampered with the little one's dosage; instead of giving the child her prescribed insulin, she gave her a brand and dosage not approved for use with children. The result was a dosage that appeared to be correct in amount but was far more potent than what the little girl needed or could handle. Marissa filled the syringe right in front of the LPN who was working with her, asking about the condition of a specific patient as she did to distract the woman. Then, when she was finished, the two women both signed the sheet verifying that all was correct and witnessed. While the LPN went from room to room with the cart, doling out the medications, Marissa waited in her office and busied herself with paperwork while waiting for an alarm or a scream, or some kind of hubbub.

It didn't take more than thirty minutes for the action to start.

Everything happened so fast, and in such a blur that it all seemed almost surreal to Marissa. Just as she planned, as soon as the chaos began, she ran from her office toward the noise. There were three nurses in the room when she arrived; one was attempting CPR on the child, the other was checking the IV and other equipment, and the third, the medication nurse, was standing off to the side with her hands over her mouth, her eyes wide and stricken.

"Go get Dr. Philips!" Marissa shouted to the med nurse on her way to the bed. She observed the nurse administering CPR for less than five seconds before demanding that the woman give her control, which took place without hesitation. As she worked, she realized that something was wrong, so she put herself into it more vigorously. "What happened here?" she asked as she went.

Hodges was the med nurse who had gone for the doctor. They had both returned within minutes, and now the doctor was shouting commands as he attempted to relieve Marissa. "Does anyone know? Nurse Hodges, had you been in here yet?"

Marissa let up for the first time ever, opting to direct her attention to the med nurse.

"I... I was just two rooms down. I had given her the after-meal shot, and she seemed fine." A tear trickled down the young nurse's cheek. "I don't know what could have gone wrong! I just don't know!"

Marissa took Hodges by both arms. "I need you to step out and pull yourself together." Marissa then turned to Katie, "I need you to take over med administration."

Marissa returned to the bed and immediately got into the swing of things, but nothing was changing. Marissa's heart began to pound harder and harder as the minutes passed and the realization that the situation was not going to be reversed started to sink in. She took over CPR once again while the doctor called for other actions, but his voice was less demanding; they both knew the girl was gone, but they kept trying.

Twenty minutes later, Marissa, Dr. Philips, and Mary stood there in silence while two orderlies cleaned up. Only seconds before the doctor had pronounced the time of death, and it was over. Marissa could hardly believe it, and her mind raced as she tried to recall the dosage and precisely what she had given so she wouldn't make the same mistake again, but adrenaline kept her from thinking clearly.

"Did Nurse Hodges say she had just been given her insulin?" Dr. Philips asked quietly.

Marissa nodded. "I helped prepare the cart myself, and we both signed off. I don't see how it could be related to her medication."

"Well," he sighed, "I'll have to check the record

myself, but I'm sure it had nothing to do with her meds. An autopsy will tell us what went wrong, but right now I think there was more ailing the girl than the diabetes issue." He looked at Marissa, who stared at the tiny sheet-covered body that lay waiting to be taken to the basement. "This is your first direct loss, isn't it?"

Marissa nodded absently.

Philips shook his head. "It's the worst. I'm sorry for you. It will be easier next time."

R.W.K. Clark

# CHAPTER 16

The death of the diabetic child threw Marissa into a confused state. While the doctors she worked with likened her mindset to that of one experiencing shock, she knew the truth on a much deeper level. Sure, she had been the cause of the 'attack' that resulted in the girl dying, but she never intended death to be a part of the situation at all. Because of that, the shock had nothing to do with it. Marissa was going through the cold, naked feeling of having lost control. Control was something she thrived on having; likely, her need for it was the cause of all the sickness and pain swimming in her mind. That need was definitely the reason she was victimizing her own patients, though she had no clue about that on any level.

Marissa, for all of her twisted thinking and harmful behavior believed that she was completely sane and normal. On some level, she thought that everyone thought like her. Yet at the same time, she concluded she was just a bit above all of those she worked around and interacted with. They were the crazy ones; they were the ones drifting through life, letting whatever came toward them have its way in their reality.

Not her; she knew precisely what she was doing, why she was doing it. She knew the need to make her stop would come, but she had no idea what that need was. Marissa was convinced she was holding all aspects of her life in the palm of her hand, and she could make any decision, carry out any act, and there would be no consequences.

The death of that girl threw all of the beliefs she held about herself and the life she had made into a tailspin, the likes of which she doubted anyone had ever experienced. Suddenly, she was out of control, and she couldn't take it back. The thought of running, as her mother had always done when she was growing up, never occurred to her; she would get out of it somehow, even if the autopsy came back showing 'foul play.' It was nothing more than a mistake, after all. Just a miscalculation.

That was her story, and she was sticking to it.

The girl's death did force her to face the hard, cold fact that she would have to stop her little game, at least for the time being. The very thought of going cold turkey made her shake inside, which in turn triggered her panic around her house like a caged animal whenever she was home. But it had to be done; she had to keep her mind off the release, off the rush she felt when she took a life… and then gifted it back and made everything that touched it whole again.

There was no power like that, none in the world.

So, the waiting game began. The autopsy was to take place two days after the girl died if nothing intervened with the procedure. The only thing that could stop it from happening would be parental intervention, but any normal mother and father would want answers. Marissa was sure that this child's parents would demand them like anyone else.

Helmsworth gave her two consecutive days off to regroup, though she didn't ask for them. He insisted that she needed to grieve. After all, this was the first time her efforts of rescue didn't work, and it wasn't uncommon for one in her position to blame themselves in cases such as these. She felt no wariness from the man, no suspicion. He purely seemed concerned that she take some time to accept what had happened as the tragedy that it was. Retribution was a small town and children didn't die in the hospital every day, especially with nurses like Marissa on the clock. She was going to have to spend some time facing it, then letting it go. At least, that's what he thought.

So, Marissa paced her home and prayed that she would get out of the trouble she knew she deserved to be in. While she knew she would have to quit, she didn't face the reality of it or consider it at all during those two days; she was too busy bargaining with whatever deity would listen.

The morning of her second full day off, also the day the child's body was scheduled for an autopsy, she received a call from the hospital at 9:36 in the morning as she paced around with a cup of coffee gripped in her hands.

It was them, she just knew it. The autopsy was

complete, and they had found more insulin in the child's tissue than there should have been. For the first three rings Marissa just stared at the phone, sure she wouldn't be able to answer it. On the fourth ring, she forced her hand, put down her cup, and picked up the phone.

"Hello?"

"Good morning, Marissa. Cliff Helmsworth. How are you feeling?"

His voice sounded as ordinary as ever, but she kept her focus on his tone, just in case she could hear deception in it.

"I'm good. Good morning to you." She gave her reply in a voice that was a bit bright, yet still apprehensive. "I think I'm doing quite well, considering. I've been thinking a lot about the child's parents, wondering how they are coping and keeping them in my prayers."

Helmsworth cleared his throat. "Well, they are one of the reasons I called you. Yesterday evening the mother and the father refused an autopsy. As it turns out, the mother is quite religious, and her doctrine will not allow for such a procedure. She was even against hospitalization, to begin with. Anyway, the autopsy has been canceled. Unfortunately for all of us, it looks as if we will never know the real cause of death. I'm sorry to be the one to tell you; I know you were as anxious for answers as the rest of us."

His words came at her so powerfully and filled her with such a force of relief that Marissa thought she might collapse to the floor. After a moment, she took a breath and set the tone of her voice appropriately.

"I'm not sure what to say," she started slowly. "How do they expect us to avoid problems of the same nature with future patients if we don't know what happened at all? You would think they would want that closure and would want us to learn from what happened."

"One would think, but it's all said and done now." Helmsworth's voice cheered slightly. "So, with that out of the way, you have the rest of the day to accept that disappointment. You sound as if you're better. You do plan on being here tomorrow, I assume."

"To be honest, I wanted to stay when you sent me," she replied, "but the time I've taken has proven beneficial. Thanks. I guess sometimes it's wise to heed the advice of the more experienced."

"I won't say I told you so." Helmsworth chuckled. "Say, I've got to run, so I'll see you tomorrow morning. On with the show, as they say."

Marissa was smiling broadly, though she didn't let her voice betray that truth. "On with the show."

She hung up the phone and dropped to her knees. That was a bullet she wasn't sure how to dodge, but it turned out the gun misfired. She couldn't have been more relieved. Regardless, it was a close call, and she was going to stop. At least, she was going to cease long enough for all of this to become a distant memory.

She stayed on her knees, soaking in the feelings of both disbelief and relief, for more than a half-hour. By the time she rose to her feet her legs were cramped and sore, but she ignored the sensation of pain and stood tall, then stretched as if she had just woken after sleeping for a month. With that stretch, she let go of every bit of worry and tension that had been stored up in her body for the last day and a half.

Without another second of thought, Marissa made her way directly into the bathroom and turned on the shower. She stood under the steaming hot water for a full five minutes before soaping up from her head to her toes, rinsing off, and stepping out. After shutting off the water, she wrapped a thick white towel around her body and padded into her bedroom, where she flopped down on the bed and fell directly into a deep sleep.

∞

Soon she was at work. The sun was shining through the window at the end of the hall. She was in pediatrics, but the wall hangings between the rooms in the corridor were those that were supposed to be hanging in labor and delivery. She felt frustration rising up in her throat at the incompetence of the staff at Southern State and made a mental note to give maintenance a piece of her mind for switching things up.

She was walking with purpose, the stride in her step carrying intent. Her left hand swung in time with her step; in her right hand, she toted a loaded syringe. She was heading for a very specific room, a room that housed a very ill infant. An infant who needed her services desperately. She knew, even as she dreamed, that while the child had been born in the hospital, he never should have left. His parents should have left him there with her, where he could be cared for appropriately in his fragile state.

The hallway was so quiet and empty that she could hear her rubber-soled shoes echoing off the floor with each step, which was strange. Also, it was dark and shadowy, though the sun was shining brightly through the window. No lights were on, and she could hear the distant sound of children crying.

The infant was in the last room on the right at the end of the hall. She continued toward it, though the corridor continued to get longer with each step, and narrower. Her impatience grew; she would never get there in time to help.

But the gap, indeed, was closing. Now she watched the boy's room as a man and woman stepped out of it. The woman was in tears, and the man was trying to comfort her. Their faces were bright, yet they were faceless. She didn't care who they were; they didn't belong to him anyway.

"Excuse me, I need to take care of him now." Marissa held up the syringe and pushed in the plunger just a tad, just enough for a tiny stream of the clear liquid to shoot out and then hit the floor below.

The woman's tears of grief turned to anger. "You have no business with him," she hissed. "I want another nurse."

Marissa laughed and shook her head. "That is impossible. I'm his nurse, I'm in charge of all the nurses on this unit, and I alone will oversee his care."

The woman broke free of her husband's embrace and slipped past the determined, but slow, woman easily. With tunnel vision, Marissa walked directly to the child's IV and inserted the needle into the access port. Suddenly, the woman from the hall approached, snarling and cursing. The tears that she had been shedding were gone. She came at Marissa with much more speed; her arms were extended before her, and her hands were clawed, ready for attack. Marissa drove the plunger home.

"You've killed him! You've killed my son!"

Surprisingly, Marissa saw the long blade of a knife, and realized that the woman didn't have claws at all; she was brandishing a weapon. Then the stranger was upon her, straddling her body as Marissa struggled on the floor beneath her to get away.

"I'm trying to help him!" she screamed. "I'm a nurse!"

The woman screamed, and the knife came plunging down toward Marissa's heart...

∞

Marissa woke with a start. Her freshly showered body was now covered with sweat, and her heart was racing. What had that been about? Subconscious guilt? No, there was nothing to feel guilty about. She swung her feet onto the floor and put her head into her hands.

Who was that woman? Her features, her mannerisms, even her voice had been so vague, yet so clear. It was as if Marissa had met her before. She knew for sure that she hadn't. If Marissa was gifted with one thing, it was an exceptional memory. She could remember nearly every patient she ever treated or cared for, as well as their families.

She did not know the woman; her mind had made it up.

Attributing it to the last of the stress from the death of the diabetic girl, she took a deep breath, shook her head to clear the remnants of the dream from the confines of her mind, and made her way to the shower again. One glance in the bedroom mirror as she passed reminded her she had fallen asleep with wet hair. She shifted her eyes to the clock on the way by; she didn't have to work until morning. Quickly changing her mind, Marissa donned a bathrobe and opted for something to eat and a movie on television. She would shower in the morning.

Settling in for a night of relaxation, Marissa pushed all negative thoughts from the forefront of her mind. But in the back of her brain, where guilt and hate lived, the dream continued to flash its undesirable scenes, and though she tried to ignore them, they gave her goosebumps and dread every time.

R.W.K. Clark

# CHAPTER 17

Allowing herself to act, no matter how she felt or how crazy it was driving her, was not feasible right then. Not only had the diabetic girl died just a few days ago, but time was moving very slowly. Mary Calvert had shown up at her home last night. She had wanted to discuss the death of the girl and a whole lot more.

Marissa had held her composure flawlessly, like an Oscar-winning actress. She served Mary a glass of wine, offered some cheese wedges and whole-grain crackers, and even put the stereo on low so the two women could talk. The smile on her face was gentle but permanent, and she feigned happiness at the surprise visit from her one-time-only friend.

Small talk aside quickly, Mary proceeded to delve into the real reason for her visit. "Marissa, I have to tell you something, and I want you to know that I'm coming to you from the heart. I'm also coming to you first because I believe there must be an explanation for the coincidences that I have been noticing."

Immediately, Marissa's heart skipped a beat, but she gave no clue as to the nervousness she had begun to feel. Her hand remained steady as a rock while she listened, and she sipped her wine with confidence. When Mary was finished presenting herself, Marissa didn't hesitate.

"What's wrong, Mary?" She allowed her smile to falter and even creased her forehead slightly to convey concern. "You sound like you're worried. What's going on?"

Mary took a deep breath and let the words rush out, afraid she would stop them if she didn't give them their way. "Marissa, I've been taking many things into consideration when it comes to everything that's been happening in pediatrics for the last several months. Um, I'm not sure what to think; all I know is that you always seem to be readily available to be the hero." The woman's voice faltered as her eyes searched Marissa's face; there was no change, she looked genuinely concerned and was listening intently. "I mean, I just have to ask you: You don't know anything about the rise in near-fatalities at work, do you? There are just so many…"

"Don't you mean near-fatalities plus one full-fledged death?" The look of worry had fled from her face. Now Marissa had just a slight look of disbelief. It said that she knew what her friend was getting at, and she wasn't going to take the insinuation sitting down.

Marissa stood up and walked three short steps to the bar that separated the kitchen from the dining and living areas. With a quick snatch of her hand, she picked up the bottle of wine and walked back to her chair. She had started to snap a little… she recognized that. But while she turned her back for the wine she pulled herself together; she was able to flip the switch that quickly. When Marissa turned back around, uncorked bottle in hand, she had a much softer look on her face, although her eyes-maintained confusion.

Sitting back down, Marissa began to pour. "Mary, are you asking me if I have played some diabolical part in harming the children on the unit?"

Her friend waited for Marissa to fill her glass, then she picked it up quickly and drank half of it down in a couple of chugs. Taking a breath, she replied, "I'm not asking that, not in so many words." She was nervous. That fact was obvious to Marissa; this would be easy enough. "I guess what I'm saying is that it's odd that you… you seem to be in the right place at the right time a lot. I'm not sure what that means, and I'm not accusing you of any wrongdoing. I just wonder if maybe—if not you—maybe you know or are suspicious of someone on the unit whom may be doing something. Am I making any sense?"

"Of course! Of course, you are." Marissa was the epitome of contentment, understanding, and serenity. "Mary, sit back, have your wine, and relax! We can talk about your concerns, but you are far too tense. We're friends, aren't we?"

Mary nodded nervously. "Of course, we are. I just… the more I thought about it and pieced together specific facts, I figured I should come to you. I don't think you've done anything… I certainly don't want to believe that you have. I believe you. I just had to talk to you about it." Mary seemed to be at ease for the first time since she arrived. The nervousness she had shown at the beginning, and while conversing, was suddenly gone entirely, from the way Marissa was interpreting her behavior. Marissa's statement about them being friends had brought the serenity and relaxation to the conversation that her feigned calmness had not been able to do.

"So… have you noticed anything strange? I mean, what about Nurse Hodges? Maybe she has something to do with the rise in near-deaths." Mary rotated her wine glass in her hands and then took a long gulp before beginning to spin it slowly once again. "I just… I just feel like there is some connection, something, or someone that ties the thing together. It's just too much to expect any less."

Marissa thought for a moment, her eyes distant. "I have to admit that I have never felt any reason for concern for any of my nurses, on either unit or their behavior… until Nurse Hodges, that is. Now I feel like, perhaps, I need to go over her medical records, verify signatures, and the like. It will be a full-blown investigation, but that's neither here nor there." Marissa reached over and placed a reassuring hand on Mary's forearm. With the gentle stroke of her thumb and compassionate look, she let Mary know that they would be getting to the bottom of things if indeed there was a bottom to get to. "I think that if we both keep this between ourselves, and keep our eyes especially open when it comes to the other nurses, we'll have the culprit in no time, if indeed there is one. And Mary, I am more than convinced that someone at Southern State is up to no good on the pediatric unit, just as you believe. It was a very wise decision to not go to Doctor Helmsworth, or the administrative board, for that matter."

Mary took another sip of her wine, her hand trembling slightly yet again. "Well," she stated in a matter-of-fact, yet timid, tone, "I did go to Dr. Helmsworth, at first. I thought since you weren't there, that he was the next best thing, if I shouldn't have gone to him first, that is."

Marissa felt her bowels go slightly loose as her heart rate increased. "Wh-What did you say to him?"

Mary shrugged and put her glass on the table, watching as Marissa went about refilling it. "Pretty much the same thing I said to you, but he was fairly preoccupied. He seemed to be listening to me, but he was busy jotting the first draft of an apology speech to the girl's parents. He told me to make sure to set up a meeting with him with his secretary, and we would discuss it, but I don't think he had any idea what I was talking about. That was when I thought, even if you were the one causing the streak of incidents, which I knew deep inside that you weren't, you were the next best course of action." Mary stopped and drank another half-glass of wine down, then held the receptacle out for one more fill, which just so happened to end the bottle. Marissa listened to her carefully as Mary continued while she went out to the fridge for another bottle.

Marissa struggled back and forth between two

options during the entire course of that evening. She was torn, as she listened to her recent friend spill her guts the drunker she got. She considered caving Mary Calvert's head in, dumping the body, and ridding herself of the risk of Mary continuing to run her mouth to the wrong person or people. Or, should she merely go along with the woman and agree to team up with her in an effort to nab the bad guy, if there was one.

In the end, she decided it was best to play the whole thing off. As she helped Mary with her coat, after calling her a cab and stashing the woman's car keys in a candy dish on the bookshelf, Marissa continued to think about the situation, and she focused on the emotions that accompanied each thought. As she put Mary into the taxi, she knew that one more body wasn't going to help anything. As a matter of fact, it would most likely seal her fate. As it stood right now, all she had to do today was go to work, cooperate fully with any investigation, and keep herself from doing anymore little exploits with the patients on either of her two units.

She took solace in the fact that she would not tinker with an infant or any treatment they were experiencing on the labor and delivery unit. That would have doubled the chances of her being caught. Right now, the worst-case scenario would end with her relocating and finding another town with another small hospital. If she stayed strong, and kept her hands off another child, it would be easy. It was just a matter of saying no, after all.

# CHAPTER 18

Marissa had separated her days between pediatrics and labor and delivery so she could focus her energies equally on the supervisory duties that being head nurse carried. This Monday was set aside for L & D, though she would do a lot of moving back and forth between units. For most of the morning, however, she would be diving into the paperwork that two days off had managed to accumulate for her. The truth was, it threatened to overwhelm her.

Today felt different to her for some reason. She couldn't quite put her finger on it, but she attributed the feeling to the fact that she had vowed she would do nothing more to jeopardize her freedom or job, or another kid's life, for that matter. Maybe what she was feeling was the new beginning she had promised to herself. She wasn't sure, but she felt an emotional tugging. The day would prove to be different.

First, after the morning nurses' meeting and all-around "welcome back" that she had to endure, she went to her office and tore into her paperwork. She had a good start on that by nine a.m., and the next thing she knew it was nearly eleven-thirty. With a growling stomach, she turned her back on a meal of her own and opted to make rounds and look in on patients in pediatrics. After that she would have a bite, then check charts and make visitation rounds at L & D.

The rounds at peds went reasonably well. She was able to catch up with the few patients who had been there when the diabetic girl had died. She had also met two new patients, both toddlers who were simply there with flu-like symptoms that may or may not have been associated with some level of food poisoning. They had both been at the same birthday party and neither were expected to have an extended stay.

She finished up in peds and hustled to the break room, where she bought a ham and cheese sandwich out of one of the vending machines, and a bottle of water out of another. She would eat half the lunch in her office before visiting L & D.

But Marissa barely got the first cellophane cover off the triangular sandwich container when her phone buzzed loudly.

"Nurse Thomas, emergency need in L & D... patient in advanced labor."

Pressing the red button on the phone, she replied, "On my way."

The sandwich forgotten behind her, Marissa jumped up and was around her desk and out of her office in seconds.

In only minutes after receiving the alert on her office phone, Marissa was in the delivery room where a woman named Julie Campbell was just about at the end of her labor and delivery experience. She quickly took the position, blending right in with the rest of them doing their jobs.

∞

Julie Campbell gave one final scream, a scream which left her body with the last of her strength, and suddenly it was all over.

There was a cry... a cry of mostly awareness, then anger. It was a cry that came from the very depths of the human soul, and the sound of it brought the most ecstatic of smiles to Julie's face and tears from her eyes. She had never heard a sound like it.

"He's all here, Julie," Bobby said to her with obvious tears of glee decorating his voice. "All his fingers, all his toes, and he is as pissed off as they come." Bobby laughed, and even though Julie was still in pain, she laughed with him.

"I want to see him," she said weakly, drops of sweat still dripping from her forehead down onto her nose and cheeks.

While the nurses fussed over finishing up the necessary tasks on Julie, another nurse had already cut the child's cord, clipped it, and wrapped him in a pre-warmed blanket that resembled a large towel more than anything else. The nurse handed the boy to his father Bobby, who in turn took him directly to his mother.

"I have someone I want you to meet, Zack," Bobby cooed over his son, his face frozen in a look of sheer awe mixed with love. "Here's your mom, Little Man. This is Mommy."

Gently, as though the boy were made of glass, Bobby handed him over to Julie, who paid no attention to the nurses still working away between her legs. She was oblivious to what they were doing. She paid no mind to the discomfort that was being caused as they worked to remove the placenta from her insides.

She took Zack, who was desperately trying to suck on his fist but hadn't the bodily control to maneuver the little hand accurately enough to keep it in his mouth.

"He's hungry," Julie murmured, glancing up at the nurse.

The nurse's eyes smiled once again. "I'm sure." The woman nodded, her eyes giving away a smile that was covered by her surgical mask. "Yes, and you'll want to put him to the breast right away. You are calling him Zack? What a beautiful name." She proceeded to assist Julie in putting the newborn to his mother's breast, trying to explain to Julie in low tones the proper way to get the child to latch on. Soon the boy was gulping for dear life.

With that, she gave Julie a nod of approval and moved away to join the other nurses, who were now finished with the placenta task and working to clean up Julie so they could get her to a freshly made bed. Then the baby would be taken to be bathed and weighed and whatever else they needed to do, and she would be taken to a cheerful room in the maternity ward.

Soon, Zack was whisked away in a rolling baby bed, and Julie was taken on a gurney to have a nice bath and put on a clean gown and other necessities. Bobby left her to herself during that time and went to the cafeteria with a ravenous appetite. It wasn't long after Julie was settled in that one of the nurses came into her room pushing Zack in his bed. Julie could tell by the woman's eyes that she had been the same nurse who had helped put him to the breast in the delivery room. Marissa was to be her care nurse because they were short on nurses that day, so she stopped to write her name on the whiteboard next to the room door. Next, she lifted the tiny new life out of his bed and handed him to his mother just as Julie took note, out loud, of her name from the whiteboard.

"Marissa," she said as she took Zack into her arms. "What a pretty name."

The nurse's eyes automatically went to the name badge, then the whiteboard, before chuckling softly. She looked back at Julie with a slight blush to her cheeks. "When my parents named me, they were trying to be unique. It didn't take long for half the world to get the same idea if you know what I mean."

Julie nodded and smiled. "So, Marissa, do you have any kids?"

The nurse's smile faltered, but only for a fraction of a second, and she shook her head. "Work keeps me busy enough; just the thought of trying to invest time in a relationship is exhausting. Besides, the little bugs here are sort of like my children; I love every single one of them."

Julie studied her face as she smiled back. "Well, you never know. Maybe someday, huh?"

Marissa shrugged her shoulders, broadened her smile, and changed the subject quickly.

Julie got an uneasy feeling about the nurse's easy blow off of the baby topic as if she hadn't been told the entire truth. Whatever it was, though, it was none of her business. If the woman didn't want, or couldn't have, children, what was it to Julie? Then, suddenly a chill ran down Julie's spine as she broke out with goose bumps over her body. The uneasy creepy feeling that came over her might actually be anxiety, Julie thought to herself. Quietly she tried to ignore the uneasiness which was so hard to pin down.

"Well," Marissa said with a sigh, and what Julie would have described as a bit of restless nervousness, "It's time for you two to get to know each other. I'm going to let you two be, and if you need anything just press the button on the stick clipped to the pillowcase; I'll be right here. One of us will come in about every half-hour anyway, as per procedure, just to make sure all is going well and take both of your vitals. Oh, and when you're ready to nap and believe me, that will come, just let us know. We'll be glad to give you a break."

"Thanks," Julie replied. "My husband will be up soon, and I'm sure he'll want some time with Zack as well. Thanks, Marissa."

The nurse slowly backed out of the room, almost as though she struggled to take her eyes from the new mother and baby; it made Julie feel a bit odd, so she offered one last smile and turned all of her attention to her son. Soon, the woman was closing the door behind her, leaving mother and child to themselves.

Julie sat on her bed, snuggling the tiny boy and cooing over him, her body rocking back and forth gently to comfort him, though he wasn't fussing in the slightest. She smiled at her own behavior, knowing that she was simply getting in some practice. She stared at his perfect face, hands, and fingers. She wanted to count every hair on his head and found herself stroking it with the tips of her fingers instead.

"Could you be any more perfect?" she asked him as he blindly worked his tiny fist into his mouth, searching unknowingly for her breast. "Could God have given Daddy and I a more perfect boy? Hmm?"

As if on cue, Bobby walked into the large private room, his smile huge as he tried to close the heavy wood door without making a sound. Julie turned to him, her eyes fogged over with love. As he made his way to his wife and son, he took in her glow and reveled in the feeling of pure bliss that coursed through his being.

"Do you want to hold him?" she asked.

Bobby bent down over them both and held out his hands, which now seemed massive in comparison to the tiny body he was taking from his wife.

The couple spent the next twenty minutes oohing and aahing, raving to each other over the magnificent job they had done making the little human being, Zack. Both of them agreed, even as he started to fuss in hunger that they would always love him, and they would protect him no matter what. They would make sure that no one ever hurt the child, and he would have the best of everything, no matter what it took.

The two of them had the boy's life planned down to meticulous detail. Bobby made an excellent living as an aeronautics engineer, as opposed to his wife's meager income as an elementary school teacher. He would work and provide for the family while she stayed home and provided the steady, ever-present parent that children so desperately needed. The boy would be home-schooled in preparation for choosing an illustrious college, and they would guide him step-by-step on life's journey, preparing him to become whatever he wanted to be in life in order to contribute to the world in a positive, and lucrative, manner. He would be their only child so they could pour all of their efforts and energies into him alone, but they would see to it that he made lots of friends, the right kind, from the very start. His upbringing would be their legacy to him, to be passed on to his children, and his children's children, allowing them and their love for Zack to live forever through their offspring.

# CHAPTER 19

A pang of confusion came over Marissa, as she relived the moment. The woman looked just like her mother. At least, she did when she smiled. Of course, it was difficult to tell how much she looked like her mother when she was wearing a paper cap on her head, but once Marissa noticed the resemblance, there was no shaking it out of her mind.

Outwardly, Marissa was all business; but inside, she was a trembling mess. Her eyes continued to shift to Julie Campbell's face, and at one point, when one of the nurses removed her paper cap, curly hair tumbled out… the woman could have been Caroline Thomas' twin sister. Marissa wanted to throw up.

Tearing her attention away from the woman and letting the nurse next to her take over, Marissa reached over quickly to attend the child that the other two nurses were cooing over. She cleaned the child with gentle haste, and swaddled the child in warm, hospital-prepared blankets that were close at hand, before handing him gently off to his overwhelmed parents. She watched as the parents went about coochie-cooing over their newborn, and another nurse, a regular on L & D, nudged her.

Marissa snapped out of her reverie. The father, Bobby, was beside himself, overjoyed with love and full of the experience. As he and his wife spoke together over the tiny new life, who was rooting around for the breast like mad, Marissa smiled and stepped closer to the small family.

"Is this your first?" She asked sweetly, masking the disruptive gurgling of hate deep inside of her, hate that she could swear was audible to everyone in the room. Without waiting for a reply, Marissa tried to continue, but Bobby jumped in. "Zack Campbell. Zack was my father's name, and we thought he would have been pleased to have a grandson named for him."

The nurse's eyes smiled once again. "I'm sure." The woman nodded, her eyes giving away a smile that was covered by her surgical mask. "Yes, and you'll want to put him to the breast right away. You are calling him Zack, then? What a beautiful name."

Julie smiled and nodded, then began to watch and listen as Marissa helped the small baby latch on to the breast. "Now, you may have something of a struggle at first with the breastfeeding. For instance, he may have trouble latching on, though he seems to have caught on quite well. You may also experience sore, chapped nipples, which is very common. There are excellent creams for this issue; we'll make sure to give you some to take home with you just in case."

The father nodded. Bobby Campbell was so enamored with his new son that he wasn't hearing a word Marissa was saying.

Marissa chuckled, "Go ahead and get the infant and mother going on clean-up. And we need his vitals and initial testing done." She stated firmly stepping away from the happy family. While she worked with the other nurses, she would glance at Julie Campbell out of the corner of her eye. It was eerie, the resemblance between this woman and her own mother. The very sight of her caused Marissa's back and shoulders to tense up with both fear and anger. The anger she understood, but she couldn't quite understand the dread. She was a grown woman, independent and self-sufficient; she had absolutely nothing to worry about when it came to the strange new mother. But the fear kept tugging; it just kept pulling away.

At last, little Zack was taken for a full bath, as was Julie, while Bobby left to find the cafeteria, or wander about, whatever suited his fancy. Before long, Julie and her new son, both fresh and clean, were in the private room that had been assigned to them. Marissa was to be the woman's attending nurse, due to the unit being short-staffed. She didn't mind. She would get to talk to the woman a bit, and perhaps dispel the unsettling feelings she was harboring inside.

Once all the red tape was taken care of, Marissa fetched the tiny, baby and pushed him in his little bed to his mother's room. Julie was waiting anxiously, and upon seeing him, proceeded to sit up, a little too quickly, perhaps. This did not escape Marissa's attention.

"You'll want to take it easy, no matter how good you feel." She handed the boy over gently, then pushed his little bed off to the side. When she returned she handed Julie a clean cloth diaper for burping. As she walked around the room, she made notes in Julie's and the baby's chart and saw to it that Julie was familiar with where the bathroom was, the call button, how to run the television, etc.

But while she did these things, she struggled to keep her eyes to herself. It was Julie who held her attention, not the baby, she just couldn't get over it; the woman's face was too creepily similar to that of Caroline's… Caroline… the Monster. It was difficult to not stare, and Marissa noticed the mother, Julie, giving her odd looks as she caught the stare on two occasions. Marissa quickly tried to busy herself with explaining to the patient how the unit worked while she placed clean baby blankets into the warming machine.

When she was finished, she turned to Julie and smiled. "Well," Marissa said with a sigh, "It's time for you two to get to know each other. I'm going to let you two be, and if you need anything just press the button."

# CHAPTER 20

Marissa's demeanor was beginning to leave a bad taste in Julie Campbell's mouth, not to mention her returning every half-hour was ridiculous. It was entirely reasonable for the mother to need plenty of sleep after giving birth. Besides, the doctor told her she would be staying for three days post-partum simply because of a blood sugar concern at the end of her pregnancy. They would want to monitor both mother and child to be sure that all was well before releasing the patients to go home. She might as well get used to leaving him with the nurses right away; Bobby wouldn't be able to stay night and day. As it was, he would be returning to work tomorrow morning.

"Did your husband leave for the evening?" Marissa asked as politely as she could muster.

"No, not yet, he just stepped out. He is certainly going to try to spend as much time as he can with us," Julie said, "but in the meantime, I really need to pee."

The two women chuckled lightly, and Marissa placed Zack snuggly in his bed before helping Julie to the bathroom. There, she assisted her by giving her the iodine wash and explaining its use. She also pointed out the bin of clean panties and sanitary napkins and showed her the string to pull in case she needed to call a nurse while in the restroom. After that, Marissa left the bathroom and closed the door. She strolled toward Zack and looked down at him, sleeping perfection.

How long will that last, though? Marissa thought to herself. The fact is, this woman who was his mother was going to cause him harm. Marissa felt it through her entire being, but as of yet had no idea what to do about it. Her mind raced as she thought of Caroline.

Marissa was enraged by the time Julie came out of the bathroom, and she had herself entirely convinced that the woman was actually Caroline; she was back on Earth and getting another chance to torture and abuse another child.

Marissa was not about to let that happen, but she needed to think. She needed time to really figure out how this could be happening. It had to be about her, about the things she had been doing. Why else would her wretched mother come back from the dead, inhabit another body, and manage to get pregnant then have the child at the very hospital where Marissa was working?

Her thoughts were interrupted by Julie attempting to come out of the bathroom, slowly and showing a bit of pain on her face.

"Mrs. Campbell, let me help you." Marissa rushed over to the woman and gently took her by the hand to guide her back to the bed. Marissa sneered slightly as she sat down gingerly, laughing lightly at the soreness between her legs.

"It was definitely worth it," Julie chirped, but as she glanced up at Marissa, she caught the tail-end of the sneer, and she felt her stomach give a nervous flop. Her eyes darted to Zack, who appeared to be sleeping soundly. "I'd like to hold him again."

Marissa wanted to give a disgusted sigh but opted instead to smile and go to the infant's bed. In moments, Julie had the boy in her arms and was cooing over him as she leaned back into her bed and got comfortable. Marissa stood there awkwardly for a moment before speaking; she was sure the woman had seen the face she had made, and it made her very nervous for some reason.

"Well I'm going to let you two be, and if you need anything just press the button."

"Thanks," Julie replied. She continued to talk in baby-talk to the new youngster, waiting to feel Marissa leave the room, but in her peripheral vision, she could tell that the nurse hadn't moved a muscle. She just stood there, hand on the door, staring at them. Finally, with as soft a look as she could possibly give, she looked up at Marissa expectantly. The nurse finally smiled, nodded, and backed out of the room, closing the door softly behind her.

At the nurses' station, she pretended to be working on the computer, but she was really watching as Bobby Campbell entered the room with flowers and a stuffed toy. Her stomach churned with anger and genuine concern; for all she knew, both of them were a detriment to the life of the boy. He was much better off without them.

She wanted to hear what they were saying in that room. Were they plotting his demise together? Did they intend to make him sick and miserable for his entire life, as Caroline had done to her, or were they just going to kill the boy and get it over with? What if the manner they used in doing so caused him pain?

If she could have, she would have flipped on the intercom to their room, muted on her end of course, so she could hear what they were saying. Unfortunately, there were too many other nurses around, and she would never be able to justify her eavesdropping. Instead, she decided to get a step ahead of things. She pulled up the entire Campbell file and began to enter her latest chart notes while simultaneously jotting down all of their contact information. She even made notes about Bobby Campbell's job. Again she sneered, this time as she closed down their file and left the computer ready for the next user. Time to do some rounds, but she knew her heart wouldn't be in it. Her mind was shredded with concern and the need to stop whatever was happening.

Marissa was glad that Julie and Zack would be staying the full seventy-two hours recommended by their doctor. During that time, she would be able to keep an eye on the behavior of the parents. At the first sign of fishiness, Marissa would not hesitate to take matters into her own hands. She would not allow that tiny baby to be tortured with sickness, or painfully put to death, for any reason.

She knew how to take care of things right.

∞

"That nurse gives me the willies, I need you to bring my laptop right away," Julie said to Bobby with fear in her eyes. "I won't be able to relax until I have thoroughly checked her out."

"Are you serious? Now you're freaking me out." Bobby said with a shocked look on his face. "Okay, I will run home now. And by the way, work called again, ugh, I have to go into the office."

They kissed each other and Bobby kissed Zack; within minutes he left the room on a mission.

R.W.K. Clark

# CHAPTER 21

It was sunny out, with a gentle, warm breeze that Julie Campbell longed to feel on her skin. Of course, it was against hospital procedure for her to take Zack for a walk outside, but she thought it would be alright if she went out for ten or fifteen minutes.

Marissa was not her nurse that day, which gave her an odd sense of relief. She had thought about the woman and worried about Zack throughout the night, but when the sun rose to all being well and as it should, she shook off the feeling and tried to focus on doing what she had to do to get home with her son. Bobby was working that day, passing out cigars or whatever men did. She was glad for it because it would allow her some time alone with Zack, as well as time to research Marissa without disruption.

She decided to take a bath, which her nurse escorted her to. This girl's name was Cassandra. She was blond, bouncy, and very friendly. Her love for babies came out in every word she said, and Julie thought she would make a great mom someday. As she bathed, Julie started a conversation with the nurse to pass the time and make the situation a bit more comfortable.

"How long have you been here at Southern State, Cassandra?" she asked as she soaked in the huge tub and soaped up a soft white washcloth.

Cassandra gave an embarrassed laugh. "Only a year, but it's been a year I'll never forget."

"Lots of learning going on, huh?"

Cassandra shrugged, and her smile seemed to falter. "Yes, that. But so much more. I mean, I'm not from Retribution, but it seems to be a pretty small town. You know, not a ton of certain patients."

Julie was confused and had no idea what Cassandra meant at all.

"For instance, if a patient is diagnosed with cancer, they are typically referred to a larger, more specialized facility. There are exceptions, like some pediatric cancer patients may stay, but that is only if the parents don't have the means to transport the patient for chemo as needed. If there is a heart defect, the patient usually stays, but if any major surgery is needed, once again, they are usually referred somewhere and transferred. Most of the regular patients here at Southern State have conditions that can be handled using the resources we have here. So, what I mean is, most staying here aren't likely at death's door, if you know what I mean."

"Sure," Julie replied, still listening, as she soaped up.

Just as Julie thought she would, the nurse continued. "The problem is that there have been several unlikely… well… near-deaths, including one death. And all on the same unit." Cassandra was thoughtful for a moment, then added, "Don't you think that's odd? I mean, before coming here I worked in Dallas, and I have to tell you that even the largest wards and units didn't have any numbers like the numbers here."

Julie's heart began to pound, but she remained nonchalant in her actions. "That is strange," she agreed lightly. "I personally have only had the best experiences with Southern State. So, were these 'near-death' experiences, as you've called them, been confined to any one unit, or any shift?" She was trying to appear as though she was just participating in the conversation, and honestly didn't think the situation was as bad as Cassandra was conveying. After all, wouldn't there have been something in the papers, or on the local news?

"Actually yes," the nurse said lightly. "Pediatrics… all of them. But thankfully the head nurse is one-in-a-million. She was fortunate enough to be in close proximity to all the incidents and was able to save the lives of every patient… except the last one. She wasn't close enough for that one, though she did give it her all when she got there."

Now Julie's mind was spinning, and she thought of Marissa, the odd nurse who seemed to have a rude preoccupation with staring.

Cassandra continued. "Yes, if it wasn't for Marissa, who knows how those situations would have ended. As it was, the last one, the one where the patient died, was so hard on her that she had to take time off, and I've never seen her even consider a sick day or a vacation. You'd think she would, but I guess being the head nurse of both pediatrics and labor and delivery just has too much responsibility."

Now Julie was nearly in a panic. She was slowly raising herself out of the tub, so Cassandra rushed over with an oversized warm towel and wrapped it around her. Soon, she was behind a divider drying off and taking care of feminine needs before getting her gown and robe on.

"Marissa," she said thoughtfully. "Was my nurse during the delivery and the rest of the day."

"Yep, she was." Cassandra was now helping Julie put her nightgown over her head. "She's a great nurse. She came here from St. Louis a while back, and she has done nothing but improve things since she walked in the door. The doctors here treat her like she's as close to being God as a woman can get."

With her slippers securely on her feet, Julie went back toward her room with Cassandra, who promised to bring Zack to her for feeding before she went out for her walk. Now, however, the stroll didn't seem so important. St. Louis was the keyword she needed; now she didn't want to let Zack out of her sight.

As she settled on the bed and Cassandra made her way out of the room for the baby, Julie stopped her. "Have there ever been any 'near-deaths' on this unit?"

"Never," Cassandra expressed. "Rest assured, if there ever were one, Marissa would be the woman to have around."

Julie didn't agree. "Is she on duty now?"

With a quick nod, Cassandra replied, "Yes, but she alternates her time between pediatrics and here. Today is a peds day for her. But don't be surprised if she stops in; she makes rounds on both units daily."

Cassandra left, and immediately Julie's eyes shifted to the clock on the wall as she pulled her laptop out of its pouch. It was only 10:30 in the morning. Bobby wouldn't be off until 4:30… she didn't know if she could wait. That strange woman gave her the heebie-jeebies; how could she be the head-nurse of two different units? Julie intended to tell the doctor she wanted a transfer, or that she would go home with a hired nurse in tow. She had no intention of giving any nurse the opportunity to harm her child, or even herself.

She fretted there alone until Cassandra returned with Zack, then she pushed the situation from her mind quickly. The baby didn't need to feel her stress, so she had to let it go. Julie would worry about making changes a little bit later.

∞

After her nurse brought Zack in for his mid-morning feeding, Julie wouldn't let him leave the room again. For the rest of the morning and throughout lunch, Cassandra tried to give the woman a break, but Julie simply wouldn't have it. At first, she was very polite in her refusals, but with each new offer to take the child, she became more and more snappy, even aggressive, and finally, Cassandra began to take it personally. She fetched the physician on duty, Dr. Stein, who tried to reason with Julie, but to no avail. Finally, he told the nurse to let them be. He let Julie know that the nurses would be coming in regularly for vitals from them both, and he also made sure she promised to use the call button if she needed anything, anything at all. It was of grave concern to him, he let her know, that she was feeling so distrustful. He touched base with her regarding post-partum depression and made sure to ask her a few in-depth questions about her mental and emotional state before leaving the room with Cassandra as Julie wished.

Once in the corridor, Dr. Stein took Cassandra by the arm as they walked toward the nurses' station. "Tell me, was there anything she might have overheard or seen that could have brought on this reaction to hospital care?"

Cassandra shook her head, a look of genuine confusion on her face as she went over the morning quickly in her head. "I took her for a nice bath, and we talked in there. There was mention of the incidents that took place at pediatrics, but I reassured her that we have the best team of nurses and that Nurse Thomas was simply the best around." She conveniently left out the fact that she had been the one to start the conversation; she knew that spelled nothing but trouble.

The man groaned. "Must have gotten to her through rumors that were negative, because the local papers have kept it heroic, which all of the situations were." He paused. "With the single exception, of course. Okay, tell you what: Make sure to keep the conversation constantly on the positive. With the erratic sugars she had toward the end of gestation, we need to keep mother and baby right here for the full three-day period.

We need to make sure that the baby has no reaction to the mother's health issues, not to mention the fact that we need to monitor the woman's sugar often. We need to keep them here until tomorrow afternoon, so just be light, carefree, airy, and above all else, professional."

"Um, Dr. Stein?"

"Yes?"

Cassandra shifted her weight from one foot to the other nervously as she glanced around to make sure they were out of everyone's earshot. "She was particularly concerned about Nurse Thomas. I mean, she never said that in so many words, but she seemed very stiff when I mentioned that Marissa did double rounds and would stop by to say hello. She has also seemed very jumpy since this morning like when I opened the door to her room, she was not only holding the baby, but she was almost in defense mode. When she realized it was me, she relaxed greatly. Do you think that perhaps she and Nurse Thomas had some kind of a…? I don't know. Maybe Marissa just rubbed her the wrong way."

Stein thought quietly for a moment. "You know, I mentioned to Dr. Helmsworth that I thought Thomas would need more than two days off after what she has been through. Perhaps she was a bit short with the patient for some reason. The best way to find out is to ask her. She's on peds today, you say? I'll go to my office and give Helmsworth a call immediately."

R.W.K. Clark

# CHAPTER 22

Marissa had just finished up after-lunch rounds on the pediatrics unit; it usually took until about two, since after-meal vitals and the like had to be attended to. Today, however, it was only 1:15. She was more than happy to be back to her office. It was a beautiful day, and she thought she might enjoy a vending machine salad out in the courtyard when she was done catching up data entry on the charts.

Her phone buzzed, and she rolled her eyes dramatically. So much for her plans. She was a bit perturbed, as she intended to invest all of her thoughts to little Zack Campbell and what she was going to do to help him.

"Marissa? Dr. Helmsworth."

Marissa picked up the receiver and punched the red button to take the call off the intercom. "Good afternoon, Cliff," she greeted. "How can I help you?"

"Have you had your lunch yet?" He asked. "I know you run late for meals with both units to attend to. I haven't eaten myself, so I thought we could break together. There were a couple of things I wanted to go over with you."

Immediately, Marissa thought about inventory or heading a surgery with him, something run-of-the-mill. "Sure thing. Do you want to meet in the cafeteria, or would you rather just grab your lunch and meet outside?"

"We can meet in the cafeteria, right at the door, by the vending machines," he replied. "I must tell you, it will sure be nice to get some fresh air. I've been gazing out my window all day. So, see you in fifteen, sound good?"

Marissa agreed and hung up the phone. It was a five-minute trip to the cafeteria, so she had ten minutes to jot down simple notes she needed to remember regarding her plan with Zack, which would take place that very night. She had reviewed, ever so carefully, both the mother's charts and medical history, as well as the brand-new one being kept on the child. She thought she knew precisely what she was going to do, so she wrote only two partial sentences to jog her memory and get her back on track later.

Tossing the pen on top of the tablet of paper, Marissa grabbed her sweater and purse, turned off the light, and closed and locked her office behind her.

∞

Dr. Helmsworth was waiting by the entrance to the vending area inspecting his fingernails when she arrived, but as soon as he noticed her, his nails were forgotten.

"Good afternoon again, Clifford," she replied with a warm smile. "We haven't taken lunch in some time, so this is something of a surprise. I hope the topics you want to cover are as simple as an inventory issue or miscounted bedsheets."

Helmsworth laughed heartily. "No, though those things will make good excuses in the future for lunch. I'll have my secretary make notes of those for me."

The pair joined the line of diners filing into the cafeteria, both of them still smiling. "So, what did you need to go over with me, Cliff?"

Now she caught his smile faltering, but only slightly. "Oh, now Marissa, nothing big… nothing big at all. First, let me get a look at you."

With a smile, she turned to face him. He quickly looked her up and down, then stopped at her face and looked into her eyes so profoundly she thought he might be reading her mind. The thought made her paranoid and put her on the defensive.

"What, Cliff?" She blushed slightly and let her eyes look at others around them, not wanting anyone to get the wrong idea. "You're embarrassing me!"

The older man chuckled, amused by her reaction. "No, seriously. I just want to know how things are going since you've come back. Anyone can say, 'oh, it's just great,' but not everyone can fake the appearance of one doing 'great.' You understand."

Marissa nodded. "Sure. So… what's the verdict?"

"Well, I'd say you look as crisp and professional as ever." He stopped to clear his throat, and his eyes got a bit distant as if he were choosing his words carefully. "But your eyes and face tell me another story."

Suddenly, a knot the size of a softball seemed to

form in Marissa's stomach. Had he been reading her mind? Had he been looking into her gray matter and deciphering her very thoughts? What if he had some idea that she had plans regarding little Zack Campbell and his… parents.

"Well," she said slowly as they advanced in line, "what are my eyes saying to you, Dr. Helmsworth?"

"I guess I see a woman who is tired; one who has worked so hard for so long that the incident only days ago was the straw that broke the camel's back." He laid a gentle hand on her shoulder. "I'm just not sure that coming back so soon was a great idea, and I feel terrible for pressuring you." He inspected her closely in silence before asking, "How are you really, Marissa?"

Her nerves let up a bit; he was merely concerned about her well-being after the trauma of the little girl's death. But the knot in her stomach remained because everything led up to something else. This conversation was only beginning.

They moved up a bit more. "I'm actually perfect, Cliff. I feel like I slid right back into things, much more smoothly than I anticipated. The unit has few patients, which is perfect. I have been able to touch base and get caught up with the little ones, who seem to be showing remarkable improvement, and I have gotten to know two very bright little people who have nothing but playing and dodging their naps on their mind. Not to mention the birth of a perfect little fellow in L & D, a boy named Zack. Yes, I'm good. Maybe tired, but good."

"Marissa, it was along that very line that I…"

Almost as if she knew what was coming next, she cut him off. "I'm doing salad, Cliff. How about you?"

He laughed. "As terrible as it really is, I'm going for the burgers and fries today… maybe a slab of cake. Patsy would kill me if she could see me, but fortunately, she's at a women's rotary meeting and couldn't make it."

The two of them shared a good laugh, then went their separate ways so they could get their individual lunches. They met at the exit, food trays in hand, and went through the short glass tunnel that led out to the hospital courtyard, with its designer concrete benches and tables, two abstract statues that had been donated by appreciative patients, and exceptional landscaping, which was very conducive to peace and deep thought.

It was easy enough to grab a table; they were the only other pair out there. Choosing the table furthest from the other people, they sat down and spent the first several minutes in silence, preparing their food for consumption. Both had chosen bottled water, so they didn't mess with the drinks right away.

After their first bites, Helmsworth spoke first.

"It seems there is a patient in L & D who is refusing to allow her newborn to be with any nurses unsupervised," he began, dipping a fry into way too much ketchup as he spoke. "Dr. Stein was brought in to speak with the woman, but he couldn't get her to listen to sense."

Marissa took a sip of water to wash her food down.

"You know, maybe they should let her see the other infants and how wonderful the care is that they are receiving. It would help her to relax a bit."

Cliff wiped his mouth with a napkin and pushed around at his burger with his forefinger, his eyes on the chocolate cake. "Well, this particular patient is mandated to remain under care for the full seventy-two due to blood sugar issues late in gestation. You know the one… Julie Campbell."

"Julie Campbell?" Marissa put her plastic fork down and looked at him in disbelief. "I was in delivery with her and then in charge of her care afterward until the end of my shift yesterday. She, um, seemed fine to me." Marissa was thinking hard now, trying to recall any of Mrs. Campbell's words or gestures that may have told her something. Other than her own suspicions, she could think of nothing. It is Caroline, and now Caroline was going to start making trouble for her somehow.

"Did she say why she is so protective over the infant? Did she see something done by a nurse that made her uncomfortable?"

Helmsworth held up a finger to let her know to wait while he chewed. With a big swallow of water, he finished his bite off and replied, "It seems that while she was bathing yesterday morning, she and her escort nurse were conversing. Somehow, the topic of the 'near-deaths' here got brought into the situation… as did, I'm afraid, your name."

Panic came over her faster than a strike of lightning. "Does this woman think I would ever consider harming a child… her child? Did Dr. Stein, or the escort nurse, try to explain that I helped the children, that I never harmed them?" Her hands were trembling, eyes were wide, and her heart was threatening to explode. Dr. Helmsworth noticed, and he wondered if lunch in the courtyard had been such a good idea.

"Marissa, relax. Both of them did, but that did nothing to sway the woman, which is why Dr. Stein is considering PPD. Maybe she's down, maybe even feeling like she may have to hurt the child before anyone else does… it could be many things. But in the meantime, Stein would like you to pay the woman a visit… with someone in your presence, of course. You could ask how she's doing, offer your hand to help. You could try to find out if perhaps anything you did or said made her uncomfortable, and if so, reassure her that the women and children you care for are your top priority. I plan to pay her a visit before her release tomorrow, just to make sure that she is going to be okay. But do that for me, will you? Maybe first thing when you head to L & D after lunch for your rounds."

Marissa took a deep breath; her appetite was gone entirely. "Absolutely, I wouldn't consider doing anything but meeting with her. Who would you recommend I take with me."

"I was thinking Mary Calvert. She knows you so well, and there was a time you two were… close."

Gathering up the hardly-touched salad and water bottle, Marissa stood. "Thank you for coming to me. I will take care of this immediately. As a matter of fact,

I'm going to speak to Mary right now."

"I've already spoken to Mary," Helmsworth said with a smile. "She's likely waiting for you now."

∞

Julie nestled Zack with her face and cooed a few times. She grabbed a tiny disposable diaper and other necessities from the table that was beneath the bassinette portion of his little baby bed. As she cared for her son, she thought about Marissa for a while.

True, she hadn't been able to gather exhaustive evidence on the woman, as she would have liked. But what she had found had frightened her to no end. Yes, she had worked at Sisters of Compassion before coming to Southern State, and yes, she had tendered her own resignation. According to what few, scant records she could get her hands on, the only thing she could tell for sure was that the departure had come after a small series of patients in her care nearly dying before being brought back to life by the woman herself. She was briefly celebrated, but a small group of parents weren't buying into the situations being all coincidental. They came forward and made demands, but instead of her losing her job, she was quietly asked to resign. At least, that was what Julie read from the parents group blog posts that finally happened.

What confused her the most was that the hospital there gave her such grand recommendations. This bit of information she discovered in the Retribution Herald. Because she was immediately hired as the head nurse to pediatrics, the small town had a big story on their hands.

She had actually made a corner of the front page.

She became a hero again and again, but very recently, a little girl died that she had been trying to resuscitate. She was given a couple of days off to regroup, and now she was back. The problem in Julie's mind was the thing that kept her from merely turning her in for investigation right then: Marissa had been nowhere near the girl when the girl had coded.

Technically, it could just as much be a matter of Marissa having a knack for being in the wrong place at the wrong time as anything else. After all, her co-workers and understaff loved her, and if you spoke to any other patients, they all had nothing but raving reviews about the cute little nurse that was so caring, yet so business-like.

Then there was the business with the cheating fiancé. Cassandra had spilled this little tidbit while taking Julie's vitals earlier that very day. Maybe, Julie thought, I am overreacting. Perhaps she was so grief-stricken that she just came off as odd.

It didn't matter. In Julie's mind there was only one way to find out, the situation was way too critical to not at least try. She had to confront the woman one-on-one. She had to be in the same room as her, and she had to see if the discomfort and disease persisted when Marissa Thomas was face to face with her. She had to see the look on the woman's face for herself when the insinuations were made, and then she would know. And she would trust no one to do it for her.

# CHAPTER 23

Marissa's pace was almost ridiculous as she made her way back inside and toward the pediatric nurses' station, where she would likely find Mary Calvert. On the way, she stopped and dumped her lunch in a garbage can in the hall, then she continued on. Before she got to the station, she saw the door to her office and made a spur of the moment decision to pop in and get rid of her purse and sweater. It would also give her a moment to think.

She wouldn't know for sure, but once she had paid a visit to Julie, she would know once and for all. The escort nurse may have just riled the patient up with the gossip, and since Marissa had made her somewhat edgy the day of the birth, the woman's overprotective mother's mind kicked in.

Or the woman was her mother Caroline after all, and she wormed the poor nurse into the conversation about the near-deaths to begin with. If this was the case at all, it was the worst-case scenario, and it meant that Marissa would have no other choice than to act and act fast. She refused to let Caroline get her stinking rotten, sickness-inducing hands on another child... ever.

But there was only one way to find out.

She quickly checked her face in the small wall mirror, put a wisp of escaped hair back into place, and put on a quick stroke or two of mascara. Then it was time to find Mary. She left her office locked and took a right to the nurses' station. She could hear her old friend's voice before she was within ten feet of the area.

"I don't know, but Jeanine from L & D said that the woman won't even take her hall walks unless the child is with her. And when she naps, she keeps her hand right on his bed so she can tell if anyone is trying to take him out."

The voice of another nurse replied, almost in a whisper, "Sounds like the depression to me. I hope they get her straightened out before she goes home. Good thing they are making her stay for seventy-two."

Marissa had paused about three feet from the station, just out of sight, and listened. Mary made no mention of her previous suspicions that Marissa was involved, which made her feel a bit better about Mary accompanying her to Mrs. Campbell's room. She took a deep breath and presented herself to her nurses.

"Mary, could I see you for a moment?" she asked in a bright, cheery voice.

Mary jumped up right away. "Of course. I'll be back, girls. Katie, will you keep an eye on my rooms?"

"Sure thing."

With smiles, the two women made their way up the corridor toward the labor and delivery unit. The smiles were necessary, they both felt, as to deter the other nurses from thinking that anything was going on that they would want to know about. As for Mary, Dr. Helmsworth had instructed her to respond to Marissa's request as she usually would. Nothing conveying any negative emotion, as to not set off the other girls' feminine radars.

As they walked, they discussed the situation lightly about Mrs. Campbell. Mary gave her input—had to be Post-Partum Depression. She had seen a couple of cases in the past, during her nursing training in Houston. For Marissa, it was really a first, Mary rambled. It probably felt like she was being attacked, in a way.

Marissa brushed that part of her statement off thoroughly. People really didn't frazzle her in that way, and Mary knew that, though she may not be thinking along those lines at the moment. Marissa simply told her that she wanted the patient, peaceful, healing, and calm. If PPD was the problem, she wanted to be sure the woman was well before she took her child and went home.

But Mary wasn't divulging everything. The more profound truth would have infuriated her friend: She had paid another visit to Dr. Helmsworth the day after she had visited Mary at her home and got half-crocked. In fact, even though she was noticeably buzzed when she left Marissa's, Mary still had that sinking feeling and the distinct impression that Marissa knew more than she was spilling and it was in no way clouded by the alcohol she had consumed. Mary Calvert, who had been active in theatrical productions before going to nurse training, had a flair for putting on a good show, but these days she kept it regulated to using her gift for acting only when needed.

In this situation, they needed it now.

Dr. Helmsworth told her that he, unfortunately, had been a bit wary and sick from the recent death. He had suspicions about Marissa that could only be made once someone witnessed her behavior or obtained proof; they were severe allegations... career destroyers. A professional registered nurse who not only headed two individual hospital units. But acting as right-hand woman to the heads of both being accused of harming and endangering small children then resuscitating them out of selfish need. It was not unheard of; it is an atrocious condition that had caused more deaths and heartache than anyone would like to count. Munchausen syndrome by proxy (MSBP) is a mental health condition that was not to be tampered with. But he also reiterated that they must take things slowly, as to make sure they were not making a mistake.

But Mary knew that it also grieved the man deeply to be dealing with even an assumption. He acted as if the woman was like a daughter to him, and Mary supposed he felt that way. She hoped they were both wrong. She hoped that her friend was just having a difficult time with the breakup of her relationship, and probably the pressure of taking on labor and delivery didn't help the situation. She hoped that was it, and that Marissa had done nothing as horrible as they suspected.

As they approached Mrs. Campbell's room, Marissa

paused.

"Do you need a minute?" Mary asked. "Time to catch your breath?"

"No, I'm fine. I just want to show her the compassion she needs right now and not react from the defensive, you know what I mean?" If she was guilty, she had Mary snowed. That had been the perfect response.

Without waiting for Mary to do the honors, Marissa stepped up to the door and knocked friendly twice before clasping her hands behind her back and waiting. Voices could be heard mumbling in the room, and seconds later Nurse Cassandra opened the door and smiled at her supervisor and co-worker.

"Hi, Nurse Thomas," she greeted. "Mrs. Campbell has expected your visit." The girl gave a slight roll of the eyes and broadened her smile, but neither Marissa nor Mary fed into the silent joke.

"May we come in?" Marissa was wasting no time, and though her expression was as soft as her voice, she was all business.

Without a word, an embarrassed Cassandra stepped back and opened the door wide. As the two nurses stepped through, Julie Campbell picked her tiny son up out of his little bed. She covered him as thoroughly as she could and nestled his sleeping body against her chest.

"It's good to see you again, Mrs. Campbell," Marissa said. "This is one of my nurses from pediatrics, Mary Calvert. I have worked with her for some time, and I thought having someone with me would help me to tell you what I need to say."

Julie stared at her. The tight smile on her face was forced and all she did was give a curt nod. For a moment, Marissa was at a loss for words.

Finally, she spoke. "Um, Mrs. Campbell, I want to apologize if I did anything during, or after, Zack's birth that made you feel uncomfortable. I have been a nurse for many years, and the last thing I ever want is for any of my patients to feel uncomfortable with me. Any feedback you have for me will only go to better me in my position, and I welcome it. Please, feel free."

Julie seemed to tighten her grip on the baby as she tensed up. The child began to squirm but made no sound, so Marissa shifted her gaze back to the patient's eyes. Julie was staring at her with an unwavering, steely glare, but the tight smile remained.

"I'm sure you know they have Wi-Fi in this hospital," Julie suddenly said in a low voice. "It's not the best in town, but they have an incredible connection and capabilities that would surprise anyone."

Mary looked over at Marissa with a raised eyebrow; Marissa looked back, trying to convey confusion. But she knew exactly to what the woman was referring. She wanted to talk to this woman alone desperately.

She didn't have to wait long to get her way. "Could Ms. Thomas and I please have a moment alone?" Julie held Marissa's eyes as she spoke, ignoring Cassandra as she stepped out, and hardly giving Marissa time to respond to Mary's hand on her arm, asking if she wanted her to leave as well. With a nod, she told the woman she would be fine. Mary went as well. Marissa had noticed Julie's lack of the word 'nurse' when addressing her, and she felt perturbed... almost infuriated. It took her a moment to practice temperance.

"Mrs. Campbell, I am here to apologize for any offense you may have experienced because of me." She continued to smile and will her eyes to keep a soft look about them. "While I admit that I am not sure exactly what behavior has disrupted you so, I am willing to hear you out and make the necessary changes needed to enhance my professional performance."

Now it was Julie's turn to smile, and this time it was genuine. Her body betrayed the woman though; she was as tense as ever. Julie realized what a vulnerable position she was in, but she was not a woman who was used to backing down from anything. She hadn't even called Bobby to come to her side... as much as she loved him, he would prove useless. Truth be told, her dear husband was a bit of a jellyfish.

"I know all about you," she said suddenly. "At least, I am pretty sure I do." She began to tighten her grasp on the infant she held, and this started the child whining. "I spent several hours learning a few things online. Unfortunately for you, weren't you quite the little hero in St. Louis as well?"

Marissa broadened her smile, but she felt her soft eyes losing their touch. "Why yes, I did work in St. Louis... Sisters of Compassion Medical Center. Why would that information interest you... aren't we talking about a personal offense here?"

Julie began to laugh, "I know all about Sisters of Compassion," she squeezed her son tighter. Now the child was starting to make a bit of a fuss, his tiny feet and legs kicking against the blankets and the arms of his mother. Marissa was watching him closely, her eyes completely off the woman who was apparently making threats to her.

"Mrs. Campbell, the child…"

"Don't tell me how to do anything!" Her grip loosened, and she took a moment to comfort both the baby and herself.

The door to the room opened, and Mary popped her head in, concern all over her face. "Are you two all right?"

"We're fine," they replied in unison, and Mary closed the door.

Julie began to bounce the baby gently. "Anyway, this whole thing about personal offense is nonsense, and you know it. The only thing about you that offends me is what you are. My mother was like you; you didn't know that, did you? Yes, she liked to hurt me and drag me to the ER. On and on and on. I know one of you when I see you, though you were a bit hard to spot head-on. So, I had my husband bring my laptop when he came back in. I did check online, just to get another perspective of who you are. You're a good nurse. It's such a shame you are a psychotic nut job."

Julie clucked her tongue and shook her head. "After all, I'm sure they were stroked pretty good by the last place you worked. You had them all in your pocket, didn't you? Just like you do here."

Julie sat there a moment, cooing at Zack, but she was watching the woman out of the corner of her eye. It gave her satisfaction because regardless of the act Nurse Thomas was putting on, her eyes betrayed the nervousness she was feeling.

"Anyway, after I read over your education history and experience, and of course, those raving reviews, I spent a bit of time digging a little... deeper... on my laptop. You have no idea how much I appreciate free hospital Wi-Fi; the information super-highway has so many more lanes when the hospital admin police aren't limiting things. Not to mention the concerned parents' group blog."

She paused for effect, then continued. "Finding out about St. Louis was the easy part; they had that information available, of course. It's what happened there that makes you so interesting, and horrible, to me. I certainly didn't expect what I found." Julie put her hand over her mouth as to stop her stomach heaving from coming up.

"Using children to bolster your ego and impress those around you?" Julie was upset, and the tone of her voice was rising. "Don't you even see how sick you are? You belong in a mental institution. I knew someone like you once, and that person shouldn't have been allowed to live; neither should you."

Julie snorted and looked at Marissa with disdain. "You know what I learned? You harmed seven children over two years at Sisters of Compassion… seven. Sure, you 'saved' them, but you had to hurt them to get the job done. You're a monster!"

Marissa was appalled; she was counting Amanda, the first girl. That had not been her doing, but now wasn't the time to clarify. She wanted to be sick, because after all the planning, all the work, all the care she had put into the kids, Julie held everything that Marissa held valuable in the palm of her hand, and she couldn't believe it was happening.

Julie wasn't finished. "And here? God, woman! Seven more children, the last actually dying! What went wrong there? Did you time things wrong? Were you going for a bigger rush and not consider the fact that you might not get there in time? The effort to save your ass came at the price of a baby. The worst part? You've only been here a short time over a year."

"What do you want?" Marissa's tone was dull and lifeless, and almost tinged with a growl. Her smile was gone, and her mind was racing. What was she going to do? If this woman did come up with proof, she was going to prison for the rest of her life, never mind losing her ability to nurse. She was going to kill this woman.

As if Julie could read her mind, her expression turned to one of horrid realization, and she grasped her baby so tightly he cried out, then she backed more than a foot across the bed, away from Marissa, in one hop of her rear end.

"I'm going to lay it on the line," Julie began, eyes

super-charged and fixed on Marissa. "I am going to discharge tomorrow, because my health, and my mind, are fine. When you leave this room, apologies will be accepted according to everyone out there, and perhaps you should even stop by the room for a goodbye before I check out. But then, the day after tomorrow, you are going to turn in your resignation. You are going to walk away from this hospital and never go to another. I don't care if you have to pick up cigarette butts with a little-pointed stick to support yourself. I don't want you near another sick person except yourself for the rest of your life."

She paused and scooted back more. Marissa was hearing what she was saying, but more than anything she was wondering if the woman hadn't suffocated the baby she was holding. When he gave a slight squirm, she looked back at Julie.

"Mrs. Campbell, I have never harmed a patient in my life. Had you read up on me and my career as carefully as you claim, you will see I tendered my own resignation at Sisters, and I left with the highest of recommendations…"

"Yes, Yes I know. After the families of patients began to catch on to what you were doing."

Marissa's eyes faltered. She had done her homework all too well. It came down to only minutes now. Everything she had worked for, all the recognition and reward, all of the blood, sweat, and tears had come down to the next five minutes. In that time, she had only a few choices. Keep her job and fight, possibly risking exposure during the investigation process or do as Julie Campbell was demanding. Resign clean and free and go on with her life or end Julie's life right now and most certainly go to prison immediately.

The truth was, Marissa had a different plan. A plan to maintain the upper hand while fully complying with Julie's demands. An idea that would ensure that Julie Campbell would never forget the name, Marissa Thomas.

"Fine," Marissa said simply, surprising Julie immediately. "So, all is forgiven. Thank you for that. Now, I hope the rest of the stay that you and Zack experience is comfortable, and I will certainly drop by tomorrow to say goodbye. You know, Mrs. Campbell, I'm so glad I'll have that opportunity because I plan to turn in my resignation the day after tomorrow."

Two quick raps on the door were followed by the heads of Mary and Cassandra popping back in. "It sounds like things are going well in here!" Mary was always listening to the tones of the voices coming from the rooms; in fact, they all did.

"Yes, we've worked it out," Julie said as she gave the two newcomers a warm smile. "It was a huge misunderstanding. And such a disappointment; no one told me that nurse Thomas was going to be tendering her resignation in a couple of days."

Both Mary and Cassandra's mouths dropped open. "Marissa?"

She openly nodded and smiled. "We'll discuss it another time. Until tomorrow, Mrs. Campbell. Please get to feeling better soon. You'll need all your energy for that new baby, you know."

Marissa was the last one out the door, and she took her time closing it behind her. She cast a long backward glance inside at Julie, maintaining her smile, her eyes glinting as she went. Yes, she had already won.

Julie Campbell just stared after her, her heart filled with fear.

# CHAPTER 24

The look that Marissa was giving her as she left did not escape Julie's thoughts. It was a look that was almost animalistic, like a leopard that lost its grasp on its prey but was promising to come back and finish the job. It gave her chills that ran up her spine and tickled the base of her brain uncomfortably, all while leaving butterflies in her stomach that could not seem to be calmed.

It was then that she was tempted to call Bobby. She talked herself out of that quickly enough; he was under enough pressure anyway. Let him work with a clear mind and heart; she didn't want him bogged down with the cares of her and Zack. They were safe, and she had made her requests clear to the staff. She did not want to have to associate unnecessarily with Marissa Thomas, and she did not want the woman providing her or her son with care of any fashion. The hospital agreed, and now that they had their little meeting of the minds, she was pretty sure that all was going to go well. She would only be staying another twenty-four hours anyway.

Julie was more convinced than ever that she was spot on in her theory. But the proof was of the essence, and that was the one thing she had none of. She gave her the ultimatum and Marissa must definitely count on the fact that Julie meant it. She intended to call and make sure that Nurse Thomas had tendered the resignation she said she would. She also planned to regularly make sure the woman was not picked up, either right away or down the line, by a health care facility of any kind. After all, Julie Campbell knew how dangerous these people could really be.

Sitting back against her pillows, she bared her breast and helped Zack latch on before closing her eyes and continuing her thoughts. The first thing she considered was her own mother. Her own dreadful, violent, yet beloved mother.

Julie's mother had been an alcoholic and a materialistic one at that. Her father was mostly overseas on business, shaking his ass to make sure that his trophy wife and beloved daughter had only the best of everything. She supposed it was the continued absences of her father that drove her mother to the violent and insane behavior Julie was subjected to, but it was no excuse. Her mother had been a monster, plain and simple.

She didn't make her daughter ill. That would have been too easy. But she would think nothing of breaking one of her fingers so they could make a trip to the hospital. Once the woman pushed her down the stairs and gave her a concussion. Several incidences were too many for Julie to count, and several she didn't even remember. What she did remember was the way her mother's running mascara looked when the police walked her to the back seat of their car. She remembered the way her mother fluttered her tear-filled eyes at her father as they escorted her away, trying to make him feel sorry for pressing charges, but he felt no remorse. He told her in later years that when he discovered what his wife had been doing to her, he hated her instantly, and nothing she could ever do would change that.

Julie ended up traveling widely with her dad and getting her education through private tutors, and it was a life she had loved. But when she met Bobby her desires changed; she wanted a husband, children, and a home. Her father supported her decision one-hundred percent.

The thought of Bobby made her smile, so she opened her eyes and glanced at the clock. It was nearly 3:30 now, and he said he would duck out a bit early and be there to visit her at five. Looking down at her son, who was now sleeping soundly, a trickle of cooling milk gathering around his lips and threatening to drip down his cheek. Her heart warmed one-hundred degrees, it seemed.

Gently pulling him off the breast, Julie got them both cleaned up and then pulled his bassinette as close to the head of her bed as she could. With a yawn, she rested a hand on the tiny bundle and let herself doze off, keeping one ear open in her subconscious for safety's sake.

"You did so well, Marissa. I knew you would." Mary was smiling and at peace. It was never good to have any form of dissension between the health care worker and the patient. Even though she and Dr. Helmsworth had been entertaining horrible suspicions, she didn't want them to be true; she loved Marissa.

Marissa chuckled. "There was nothing to be worried about. I was nervous, I'll admit it. But it turned out to be nothing. She said I reminded her of her mother, and I guess that wasn't the most supportive relationship she's ever had. What made it so easy to deal with was the fact that my own mother and I had serious problems, you know? I was able to quickly share a bit of my story, and it put her at ease." She paused. "I did agree to not be involved in her care while she's still here, though. We want her to remain as comfortable as possible."

Mary stopped dead then, and put her hand on Marissa's arm, making her friend stop as well. "What's this about resigning?" She asked.

Marissa shifted her eyes from here to there, trying to think of the best way to answer. Mary waited patiently, not wanting to interrupt her train of thought. Marissa finally took a deep breath and spoke.

"I'm going to be making a career change," she said. "The pressure of last week has genuinely proven too much for me. When we get back to the unit, I'll be meeting with Clifford and making him aware of my intentions, and in two days I'll turn it in. Um, I'd really appreciate it if you wouldn't say anything to the other nurses; I'll do the honors when the time is right, okay?"

Mary didn't react as Marissa expected. She thought her former best chum would have started to cry, or act appalled at the very thought. Instead, she simply started to walk, slowly, her hand still on Marissa's arm.

"Are you sure this is what you want? A career change? What are you considering going into?"

Marissa shrugged and smiled. "You know, to be honest, I'm really interested in computers, so I'm looking into options in that field." Marissa couldn't help but notice that Mary seemed almost relieved. "Maybe you'll get to move up into my position."

Mary laughed loudly. "Heck no! You have more on your plate than a six-handed monkey. I'll pass. I guess I'm just surprised that you're leaving at all, but I can imagine that with all that's happened it will be a relief for you."

Mary Calvert didn't look Marissa in the eye once during that last statement, and that was when she knew that Mary was suspicious of her. Nothing she said was tell-tale, but it was all in the way she said it and in the lack of reaction at the news of her plan to leave. Well, if she was suspicious, she could bet that Helmsworth was too. Yes, it was the perfect time to go.

They were approaching the nurses' station on the peds ward, and Mary started going on about finally being off work, what a long day, and what were Marissa's plans when she got off? Marissa stood visiting with Mary and the other nurses, telling them that she was staying late to catch up some paper and computer work that was put off by her meeting with Mrs. Campbell. She listened to their plans for the evening, caught ear of some gossip from the surgical ward that was a bit funny, and then made her way to Helmsworth's office.

Her timing was perfect; he was just preparing to leave himself.

"Marissa! I'm glad you stopped before you left for the day." He had been putting on a light jacket, which he now removed. Gesturing toward his office door and telling his secretary to hold his calls, the two of them went inside and sat down.

"So, it went okay with the Campbell woman?" The smile on his face was fatherly and genuine, and Marissa wondered if she hadn't been off-base when she thought he was suspicious of her.

With a nod, she replied, "Yes, yes it did, as a matter of fact. She also invited me to see her off tomorrow. Mostly it was a big misunderstanding. Her reasons for lashing out at me were a bit personal for her, so I gave her my word I would keep them to myself. But I do intend to pop in and tell her goodbye tomorrow. She certainly has a handsome little guy on her hands, doesn't she?"

"Indeed." Helmsworth chuckled heartily. "Well, I'm glad she holds no resentments, and I hope that her reasons clear up quickly for her."

"Yes." Marissa looked down at her hands in her lap, then pretended to pick lint from the leg of her purple scrub pants. "Um, Clifford, I came to see you for another reason as well. Do you have a moment, or are you in a rush?"

"I'm fine," he said, a look of concern on his face. "Go ahead, please."

So, for the next twenty minutes, Marissa told the man she had worked so closely with that she would be resigning the day after tomorrow, and she told the same reason she had told the others as far as why. She spoke about the death of the diabetic girl, and the pressures of running two units, but insisted that those weren't the primary reasons she was going to leave. The computer training excuse sounded good, but she didn't think he looked like he was buying it. She didn't care she was leaving Southern State, and she meant it.

Helmsworth sat back in his leather chair, heard her out while doing nothing more than nodding now and then and maintaining a serious look with his fingers steepled beneath his chin. Finally, when he was sure she was finished, he spoke.

"You know, Marissa, I consider you one of the finest nurses I have ever had the pleasure of working with." He sat forward and put his elbows on his desk. "But I know first-hand the pressures that accompany the careers we have chosen; you doubled up, and you did so admirably. But I must agree with you; I think it may be in your best interest to move on. The main reason being the most important of all: for your own well-being. I'll be terribly sorry to see you go, but I want what is best for you, and for all the patients involved. If you ever need anything, please don't hesitate to come to me."

Marissa didn't even hear the last sentence; her hearing stopped at 'patients involved.' He was suspicious! And Marissa was willing to bet that if there was a way to find out, many more of her co-workers were as well. Had this situation with Julie Campbell not happened she may have been on her way out the door anyway.

As Dr. Helmsworth went on about the support available to her, and how valued she had been to his team, she thought about the Campbell woman and the way she hissed at her, like Caroline would, and the way she tried to strangle her own child right in front of her. Yes, she was going to take care of things permanently.

Helmsworth was standing now, so Marissa automatically followed suit. "So, what will you do for the next couple of days?"

She followed him to the office of his door and lightened her voice. "I'm going to catch up on things, so my relief isn't overwhelmed. It's so important to set things right before leaving a job like this, wouldn't you agree?"

Helmsworth put an arm around her and gave her a squeeze. "I absolutely agree. So, I'll expect your resignation in two days. See you then."

# CHAPTER 25

"You're kidding right?" Bobby pushed his round tortoiseshell glasses back on his nose and looked over his shoulder at the closed hospital room door. Lowering his voice, he sat down on the bed next to Julie, who was smiling and making baby noises at Zack, while alternately pretending to eat his tiny fist.

"No, I'm not kidding. Am I, kiddo? Am I? No, Mommy wouldn't kid…" motioning to Zack.

Bobby groaned. Julie always had been the stronger one, and she was the one who listened to her gut feelings more than anyone he knew. If she had a strange feeling about someone, Bobby listened to her. More times than not her intuitions panned out, and many times paying attention to them had saved them heartache.

But Bobby, himself, had a bad feeling about this. "I don't know, honey." He looked back to the door. "Don't you think you two should just check yourselves out and come home? I mean, the woman didn't agree to resign for a couple of days! What happens if she does something nuts? You know better than anyone how these people are. They are capable of anything."

Julie planted several rapid kisses on Zack's soft cheek, then handed him off to Dad and made her way to the bathroom slowly. "Listen," she said through the slightly opened door, "I believe I made the woman genuinely nervous; if you could have seen the expressions on her face, you would know what I mean. She isn't going to do anything to put her own freedom at risk. As it is, if she just gets out of the business and goes on with something else, lives are saved. I'll bet you one million dollars right now that another rash of 'near-death experiences' never happens again. The nerve! I mean, in a town the size of Retribution. And those poor kids!"

"But why not just turn her in?" Bobby was pacing with the baby now, his wheels really turning. "I mean, why even take the risk of her being around you and Zack, or anyone else for that matter. Even if she's innocent, she would have been off-duty pending the results of an investigation. No one is hurt."

"If she's innocent, why has she so readily agreed to do what I demanded?" Julie was becoming a bit worked up, though she was keeping her tone at an acceptable level. "And why did she give me that wicked, evil smile when she left my room. No, I'm right about this."

"She's probably going to sue us for slander." Bobby stopped long enough to put his sleeping son back in his bed before starting his pacing all over again.

Julie came out of the bathroom tying her robe, smiling serenely. "Listen, dear. I'm telling you that woman is dangerous. If you would just go home tonight and get on the computer, you would see for yourself. Now, the reason I am opting to stay rather than check out right now is the fact that blood sugars are nothing to mess with. I'm not so much concerned about myself, but I want to be sure that Zack is perfectly fine before taking him. So, that's that."

Bobby didn't bother to argue, and when Julie changed the subject to the fancy dinner they were going to get, with wine and chocolate lava cake and all, he went with the change. But deep inside he was a nervous wreck. The sick feeling he had been sporting sat in the pit of his stomach and gave him a sense of impending doom like nothing he had ever experienced before.

∞

More than once during their meal Julie asked him if he was okay, and when they were talking and spending quality time with Zack right before visiting hours were over, she asked him again.

"I'm fine, Julie," he replied the last time, his voice tinged with annoyance. "I'm worried about you two, but I guess that comes with the territory."

Julie rubbed his shoulder. "It's just that you've been holding Zack and staring at him for the last two hours, barely speaking. It's just not like you."

"Do you think they'd let me stay here tonight?" he asked.

Julie stared at him for a long moment, a half-smile on her face as she tried to figure him out. "You really are spooked, aren't you? Listen, I'm surrounded by doctors and nurses, and they are all aware of how I feel about having any contact that is professional or otherwise, with Ms. Thomas."

"I can't believe you gave that woman an ultimatum with virtually no physical evidence," he muttered, almost to himself.

Just then, the room door opened and a nurse came in, smiling broadly. She was slender and blond, with blue scrubs. Both of the Campbells looked up at her and smiled; Zack continued to sleep quietly, oblivious to all that was going on around him.

"Hi, you three! How was that dinner?"

"Actually, surprisingly good." Julie turned to Bobby. "What did you think, dear?"

"Wonderful. Just great."

The nurse took a stethoscope from around her neck and walked over to stand beside where Julie sat on the edge of the bed. "I just came to get the 9pm vitals from you and Zack." With a sad look on her face, she said. "I don't mean to be a stickler, and I am sorry to say but visiting hours were over at 8pm. But I do have some good news though, your physician said that after your 1pm vitals tomorrow, if all is normal, and we expect it will be, you will both be discharged. Isn't that great news?"

"Wonderful is more like it!"

The nurse went about her procedures, and while she checked Zack, the couple took note of the time and began to say their goodbyes. Julie insisted that Bobby get home early to get a good night's sleep due to his work commute. They hugged, kissed, exchanged endearments, and then Bobby took little Zack into his arms and snuggled him like crazy.

"I love you, kiddo," he told the babe. "You remember that forever and ever I will love you."

Julie watched, tears of joy in her eyes, as Bobby put the baby back in his bed, kissed his wife one more time, and left the room.

"Well I have some good news. Your doctor changed the frequency check for vitals to every four hours. So, Mrs. Campbell, all is well then? No pain that is out of the ordinary?" The smile seemed to be painted on the nurse's face.

With a shake of the head, Julie said no.

"Now, I know this is the first time I have attended to you and Zack, and I understand that during your last night, and final day, here, you have some special requests that your doctor has agreed we abide by. Is that correct?"

"Yes," she said with a yawn.

"So, first off, Zack is to sleep with you in your room. If we get to his crying before he wakes you, we are to wake you so that you can administer care, correct?" Her voice was just too cheerful, and Julie had to suffocate her annoyance.

"Secondly, you do not want to be awakened for 1 a.m. vitals, since you haven't had a good night's sleep in the last few days. Now, you do understand that, with this being your last night, the doctor wants you to know that he can't stress enough how important all vitals are."

Julie nodded wearily and pulled Zack's bed up near

the head of her own, then she lay back on her pillows and covered up. "I understand. Listen, the only reason that I haven't wanted to wake for vitals is that I'm so exhausted. But if the doctor feels better about me waking up for ten minutes and feels it will assure my going home with my son, then go for it. It is my last night here, after all."

"Oh, good! He'll be pleased with that! Then I will be back at 1 a.m., good night." She scribbled notes in her chart as Julie began to doze off; it had been one exhausting day.

By the time the young nurse was done, Julie was fast asleep, snoring slightly, as if she passed out from exhaustion. Zack was next to her bed, his touching hers, but for the first night since he was born her hand was not resting on him. Julie had no mental stress keeping her half-awake; for the first time, she had peace.

The nurse, who had read her chart thoroughly, could tell. With a smile, she moved Zack's bed out about a half-foot, so if Julie needed the restroom she wouldn't jostle the boy, then she gathered her chart and stethoscope, turned out the light, and left. Neither Julie Campbell nor the nurse realized that the final directive had been long forgotten: No Nurse Marissa Thomas allowed on the ward.

# CHAPTER 26

From the time she walked out of Dr. Helmsworth's office with him until nearly eleven that night, Marissa sat in her office, supposedly catching up on paperwork and data entry. She didn't make any rounds and she didn't talk to any of her co-workers. But for a couple of trips to the bathroom and one to the vending area for a bite to eat, she didn't make any appearances whatsoever. She simply offered a friendly smile and nod to anyone who took notice of her. They all knew who she was, and she seemed to be confining herself to pediatrics, though she doubted that anyone on this shift had received orders to keep her away from labor and delivery. That was good because her entire plan was based on that hope alone.

Otherwise, Marissa sat alone in her office, the door locked, and the lights dimmed. The screen saver bounced around on her computer, but even that didn't faze her; she was focused, and waiting for a quarter to eleven, she knew precisely what she was going to do.

Southern State was a small hospital. At night, except for an emergency or early birth, they had a bare-bones staff. Two nurses at each of the units she oversaw...

One was always doing rounds, vitals, or answering call bells. The other was typically doing minimal data entry, painting her nails, or talking to a boyfriend on the phone. Sure, all of this was frowned upon by administration, but they were all home in bed. The chances of any night nurse receiving a write up for these behaviors was slim to none.

The same thing went for labor and delivery. Marissa knew all of the procedures inside and out, and she didn't feel the least bit nervous about what she was planning to do. She knew in her heart that everything would go off without a hitch. It was the aftermath that she was counting on, though. She wanted a particular reaction to what she was going to carry out, but there was no guarantee things would work out in her favor. If they didn't, she would likely face a rash of charges, because she had no desire to cover her back. But if things worked out, well... one could hope.

At 10:45 on the dot she stood up quietly from her desk and removed a pair of jeans, tennis shoes, and tank top from her gym bag, which she kept in her office in case she had plans to go out with the girls after work some time. She started bringing a change of clothes after the night at the Mexican restaurant, though she never planned to use them... until now. She changed into the clothing, then pulled out a maroon flannel shirt and a baseball cap. She covered the tank top with the flannel, left her hair up in its typical bun, and covered her head with the hat. Next, she put on a pair of glasses with plain glass frames. Marissa often wore them to look more studious and professional around people she felt she needed to impress. It was silly, but now she saw it as preparation she had consciously known nothing about.

Marissa looked in that office mirror one last time before stuffing the now empty gym bag with a small, soft pillow used to ease the pressure of bedsores. Bending down she then pulled a doctor's coat and stethoscope from her bottom desk drawer. It fit nicely in her bag, and she only zipped it closed a quarter of the way for easy access when she got where she was going. She left her office for good, not even bothering to lock the door behind her or take anything personal with her.

"Good night, ladies," she said cheerfully as she passed the nurses' station. The two nurses on duty actually looked like they were doing their jobs for once together. "I am finally out of here for the night. I'll be back in the morning." On a whim, Marissa decided to stop and chat with the girls, striking up a casual, but brief, conversation. One of the young nurses looked up, then squinted her eyes as if she was trying to recognize the woman she was talking to. Suddenly, a smile broke out on her face, and she beamed up at Marissa. "Nurse Thomas! What a pleasant surprise! I'm working a double, filling in, but I don't mind. How about you? You're never here at this hour!"

"Oh, I got behind on paperwork and computer stuff due to all the drama as of late, but I think I'm caught up now." She held her smile. "It's good to know we have nurses here at Southern State who are willing to take one for the team when needed; I'll be sure this goes on your record."

"Thank you! So… you're heading out finally, huh?" She seemed star-struck at having the opportunity to speak with the head nurse and hospital hero.

"Yeah, finally. I was going to take the elevator and then rush to the closest margarita bar I could find, but I decided at the last minute to take the back stairs… good exercise, you know. Plus, I've put on ten pounds sitting behind my desk, not to mention my penchant for… you know… margaritas."

"I love them myself," the young nurse confided. "Anyway, it was so wonderful talking to you! Really! Have an awesome night, and don't forget to call a cab if you need to!"

The other nurse she barely knew on a personal level, grunted. "They sure do work you to death, ma'am. If they offer me head nurse, my answer's set in stone."

The other, added with a snort, "You got that right."

The three of them laughed, said their goodnights, and Marissa started down the hall without looking back. Call a cab… that was funny. She already had, and it was planning to pick her up at Las Flores, four blocks away, at one in the morning. That way she had a bit of time to fog her own mind. It would make dealing with things in the morning much easier.

Marissa had to get to Julie and Zack. She had to get to their room without raising any ruckus or suspicion. On the peds unit, both of her nurses were at the station; what if it was the same at Post-Partum Recovery? She wouldn't have any foreseeable problem passing through L & D; she had to do that to get to the elevator going down to the parking garage. But PPR was another thing entirely. Sure, the nurses would be doing vitals and rounds, but if even one was at the station, she was going to have a problem. The only thing in her favor was the lack of familiarity she had with the night nurses. Here she was in street clothes; what could she be doing there? And if she told them who she was, it would surely raise a red flag. She had been explicitly told to stay away from the Campbells and their baby. While she felt no anxiety or nervousness, she kept her fingers crossed, gritted her teeth, and proceeded to don the doctor's coat from the gym bag.

There was only one nurse at the station, and she was busily typing away on her computer. A quick glance told her that the girl was a brand-new nurse (what luck) good thing she was here.

The hall that Julie Campbell's room was in was dim, the only lights being the tiny ones that lit up the room numbers. Julie's was the third room on the right. A quick look around told her that no one was inside. With a deep breath, Marissa approached the room, took hold of the ajar door, and slipped inside without barely opening it any more than she already had. She left it open slightly so she could see from the dim hall lights.

She could see plenty.

Both mother and child were sleeping soundly. Julie was on her bed, sprawled out and snoring as if she was passed out and in a stressed induced coma, likely wiped out from the exhausting days prior. For a moment, all Marissa could see was Julie, and she was tempted to carry out her plans on the woman instead. But then she turned her focus to Zack. He was really the one she was concerned about; he was the one she was there to save.

She had to save him from Julie. She had to protect him from a lifetime of abuse and sickness and being used for attention. Only when he was in Heaven would he be free from the threat of the woman lying next to him, so she put Julie out of her mind and gently sat her gym bag on the floor. Taking the small pillow from it, she looked over her shoulder one more time, glanced at Julie, and then put the pillow over the child's face while she watched Julie sleeping soundly.

He didn't make a peep; in fact, the baby hardly squirmed. She held the pillow there tightly until, at last, she saw his tiny hands quiver in the dim light and then go limp. Taking the pillow from his face, she laid her hand on his chest. There was no rise or fall. Next, she pulled the stethoscope up and checked for a heartbeat.

The boy was dead, and one-touch told her he was already acquiring a chill.

Quick as lightning and silent as a ghost, she peeked out and, upon seeing that all was clear, Marissa went to the end of the hall like a shot. She opened the door to the fire stairs and went through, being careful not to let the door slam. Marissa replaced the doctor's coat including the stethoscope, into her gym bag, donned her ball cap and left the zipper open. She watched through the small reinforced window for a moment, just long enough to see if anyone was coming, then bounded down the stairs two at a time. She slid down the hall to the emergency department on the first floor, where she blended in like a regular citizen. Soon, she was on her way to Las Flores for her margaritas, a feeling of exhilaration and freedom that she hadn't felt in years.

Later, as she inundated herself with margaritas and waited for the time to come for her cab to fetch her, she thought about the truth. In the morning she would be visited by the police, she expected. They would arrest her, and she didn't care. Marissa understood now that her entire purpose in life was to rid the world of Caroline Thomas.

She didn't care about police, or prison, or a bad, misunderstood reputation. No, she had a much larger agenda. She wanted the first visit she got in the morning to be from Julie—Caroline herself, and she had a feeling that it would be.

R.W.K. Clark

# CHAPTER 27

Marissa made it home that night and fell asleep like a drunken log.

Little Zack Campbell was discovered deceased at his 1 a.m. vitals check. The assigned nurse didn't wake Julie, but instead went to her co-worker. Together they called the physician on call, but that was only after they slid the child out of the room and tried CPR for fifteen minutes.

The doctor arrived, and the child was officially pronounced dead. The next step was to call the father. The on-call physician insisted since he was aware of the mental state the mother had been in; having Mr. Campbell there would help ease the blow.

While the doctor and his nurses were conferring with the father, Julie woke up to go to the bathroom. When she saw that Zack's bed was gone her first assumption was panic, but after her much needed rest she then relaxed and assumed that he was having vitals done, and they had opted to spare her the wake up after all. Pleased, she relieved herself, then went back to her bed and turned on the over-bed lamp to wait for Zack's return.

The door opened, and she quickly asked. "Where is Zack?"

The nurse and her co-worker stood there, reddened eyes and heartbroken looks. Dr. Swift approached her and gently began to break the news to her. But before he could get a word out, her eyes went red, and she screamed into her hands.

He put a massive hand on her shoulder and she felt his compassion as he did so. Julie was hysterical, the tears were streaming down her face. Tears of grief and a fit of raging anger that she thought it would make her vomit all over the man with the sleepy eyes and the askew tie. Everyone immediately surrounded her to lend a hand. Within a few minutes, she was able to catch her breath. She kept herself in check by breathing slowly and waiting for him to speak.

"On first observation, I am calling SIDS. Now listen, we will have a full autopsy if that is what you want, but for now, I have called your husband. He is on his way, and then the two of you can discuss all of the details. Can I get you a sedative? Or would you like to see clergy?"

"No," she said, almost too quickly. Continuing to let the tears fall freely, Julie continued. "I just want to be alone until my husband gets here, please."

After reassuring the hospital staff over and over, that she would be ok, they finally assessed she wouldn't do anything drastic and left the room. It would take Bobby over forty-five minutes to get to her from their home out of town.

On a mission, Julie went to her closet. She chose a pair of sweatpants, a matching sweatshirt, socks, her tennis shoes, and a light jacket. Donning it, she grabbed her purse, gave a fleeting thought about changing her feminine napkin, and then opted to stuff a few out of the bathroom into her bag instead.

Marissa wasn't the only one to be aware of the fire stairs; Julie noticed them every time she walked the hall. Now it was time to take them, and she flew down them nearly as fast as Marissa had only hours before. She saw a taxi parked right outside for hire, jumped in, and asked him to drive her to the nearest store. She would tell him where else to go shortly.

Fishing her smartphone out of her purse, she nearly panicked when she saw the battery was at ten-percent. Julie knocked on the partition, which the driver had closed to avoid conversation, and smiled.

"I'm really in a bind here, an emergency of sorts," she said as he stared at her in the rearview mirror. "You wouldn't happen to have a smartphone charger, would you?"

"Yes," he rasped.

"Good! May I use it?"

The man handed her the end and then shut it in the partition door. Plugging in her phone, she began her search; she recalled seeing her physical address listed somewhere. All she had to do was enter Marissa's name, and she had everything she wanted at her fingertips.

The cab driver stopped at a Super Mart where she bought some liquid lighter fluid, a pack of lighters that were long-nosed and had a trigger. The lighter fluid wasn't for the lighter, but they would work well together. Making her way to the scant tool section, she found a pair of pliers, some thick rope and duct tape. By the time she was finished checking out, it was time to make her way to Marissa Thomas' home.

Soon, she was having the cab pull up a few doors down. With her bags in hand, Julie paid the driver, tipped him well, since she was sure he would remember the trip anyway. As he pulled around and out of sight, Julie found herself staring at Marissa's house; her lights were out. There were no cars at all parked at the residence. Didn't this woman drive, she thought?

Frozen with grief and toting her bag in her hands, she made her way to the glass-paned rear entrance. Her stomach sank at the realization that it looked secure. Her mind started to race as she tried to find the courage to break a window just to get in. But fortunately, right then, the sliding glass door gave way and slid silently on its tracks. She stopped the door with her foot and then used her elbow to wedge her way in. It was done, and she had to stand there a moment to catch her breath.

Before heading up the stairs, she looked around the house. The face of her son flashed before her mind's eyes, and for a moment she thought she would crumble to the ground right then and there.

But she didn't. Instead, she let the pain drive her up the steps. Then she would have to rethink things. With one more look up and down the hall, no sooner had the concern crossed her mind, than the bedroom door opened easily. Julie stepped into the room and softly closed the door behind her. When she got to Marissa the stench of alcohol was overwhelming. The woman was passed out on her stomach, mouth wide open, and she was dead to the world. Julie couldn't help but smile as she put her bags on the floor.

"I didn't think you'd make it so easy for me, you psychotic bitch," she said in a whisper.

R.W.K. Clark

# CHAPTER 28

"Wake up," Julie said, slapping a leather belt from the closet across the woman's legs. "I said, 'Wake up, you murderous bitch.'"

Marissa began to stir, groaned with her eyes closed, and then turned in the direction of the voice she was hearing, the sound that seemed to be invading her ears and pounding at her brain with little hammers.

"Wha—Who?" She tried to focus her eyes, and then recognition came into them all at once, and Marissa laughed. "Julie! It's good to see you! I knew if I sent Zack home I could get you alone, and now we can battle this out together."

Suddenly she felt the most searing pain she had ever experienced. It was at the sole of her right foot, and it instantly froze her scream and brought tears to her eyes. Marissa began to struggle, then struggle harder. Suddenly she realized she was tightly tied to a chair, her wrists and ankles bound tightly.

Burning on the sole of her other foot hit her like a brick wall, and this time she was able to scream like a banshee.

"There is no one here to hear you," Julie taunted.

"And thanks to the sound-proofing in the house, no one outside can hear you either." Julie then drove a glowing red-hot knife tip into her ankle, this time holding it there while it sizzled.

"I have to thank you for not making Zack suffer. I know what suffering is all about." Julie removed the hot metal tip of the knife to save it for later. "My mother used to break my bones, so she could hang out at the hospital." She lit the lighter, then grabbed Marissa's face with her other hand and jerked it hard, so they were looking each other in the eyes. "I know all about you, you sick, mentally deranged lunatic. You're a walking example of Satan."

Suddenly, it occurred to Marissa why there had been recognition: she saw the look of a victim and mistook it for the look of the perpetrator. In Julie's case, the exact opposite applied, only Marissa had transformed from victim to predator and Julie knew it.

Julie brought the flame closer and closer to Marissa's left breast. Marissa was terror-stricken, and she began to fuss and shake in the chair, fighting with all her might. Julie lifted Marissa's left bosom in her hand and held the lit lighter to the soft tissue under her bust. The sound and smell of sizzling flesh filled the air. Marissa's screaming was deafening, but Julie continued to hold the lighter lit till Marissa passed out.

∞

Marissa's eyes began to flutter, she woke with excruciating pain under her left breast, and her head was spinning. She frantically looked around the dimly lit room hoping, praying Julie was out of her house and out of her life for good, that she had simply left her bound to the chair.

Dawn was slowly approaching, and soon she would be able to see clearly. Blinking her eyes and shaking her head, Marissa tried hard to focus her vision. That's when she noticed in the distance a strange orange glow. With more concentration through squinted eyes, she saw the glow was moving, and it was coming towards her. It was Julie holding a red-hot knife. Marissa began to scream once again, at the top of her lungs, but it was short-lived and ended quickly with coughing and choking from her hoarse throat.

Within seconds Julie was upon her pressing the red-hot glowing knife to Marissa's right arm. The sound of flesh crackling in Marissa's ear made her head swim. Julie continued to apply pressure to the blade waiting for Marissa to lose consciousness.

∞

The pain of Julie picking and prodding cruelly at her burnt, peeling flesh yanked her back to reality with a scream, which she muffled in the pillow. Julie laughed at her and stopped as she stood up from the edge of the bed. Marissa raised her head slowly from the tear, spit, and blood-soaked pillow and looked at the woman out of the corner of her eye. Suddenly she realized she was naked, tightly bound and duct taped, spread-eagle, to the four-poster bed.

Julie was twirling around, slowly, humming lightly and blissfully to a song that Marissa just realized was playing in the distance. Julie had the living room stereo playing, and as her head cleared, Marissa realized she had it cranked up pretty loud. Without a doubt, the bound nurse knew that the woman had not only lost her mind, but she was also humming and seemingly doing a ballet dance to an alternative rock song. Then she saw the pliers in Julie's right hand.

They had red rubber grips that almost made the tool appear to be dripping in blood. Julie had a firm grip on them, and as she danced she would drift to the bed and away from it, menacingly jabbing the nose of the pliers at Marissa's ears, nostrils, and neck. Marissa was experiencing true fear.

No sooner did the question cross her mind, than the radio jock began jabbering about some brand of hoagie sandwiches. "Oh! I almost forgot what I was doing!" Julie giggled hysterically as she left the room at a light jog. Suddenly, the radio got even louder, and Marissa knew that it was a very bad sign.

"Can you hear me, Marissa?" Julie was back bending over the bed, her face only inches from Marissa's stinking, burnt arm. "I sure hope so, because I have a lot to say, but we don't want anyone else to hear, do we?"

Marissa knew no one else was home; she knew her neighbors and their schedules, as they knew hers. The radio was unnecessary, but Julie would never buy it. Marissa buried her face in the pillow again.

"No! You don't get to hide! You don't get any breaks!" After grabbing the back of Marissa's neck and jerking her head up for eye contact, Julie held the pliers up and turned them around before her eyes, giving her a good look at them. "See these? These are the healers of your malady. This is the prescription; it is the creditor that is coming to claim its debt. You should expect retribution to be swift and painful. Yes, I seek retribution for fourteen children… that means I take fourteen from you. Fourteen… and nothing else matters!" She screamed out the line to the song, then spun around, dancing a bit more for effect.

Marissa asked her a question, but her throat was raw and hoarse.

Julie, who saw her lips moving, bent down and asked, "What did you say? You're sorry, perhaps?"

Marissa flashed an evil smile with her lips and shook her head.

Julie narrowed her eyes and knelt next to the bed. "Then what did you say?"

"I asked you, fourteen what?" Marissa spat.

Julie began to laugh hysterically, but it stopped abruptly as she looked Marissa in the eye and giggled. "Why, fingernails, of course. One for each of those helpless children that didn't belong to me, one at a time, extracted with Mr. Pliers here."

A look of horror came over Marissa's face. "Don't worry," Julie said, her face nearly pressed right against Marissa's. "After the first—I am guessing five or so, you'll be passed out from the pain, and you won't even feel the rest not to mention the last six I take for Zack's sake. That's likely a relief for you, but I get no comfort from it at all."

In the blink of an eye, she quickly stood, sat her ass down on Marissa's bound right arm, and took the duct taped hand in her grasp tightly. The woman tried to squirm and pull it away, but the attempt was futile. Before she knew it, Julie had the tip of her thumbnail grasped tightly in the pliers. She turned to Marissa, smiled, and said, "On three, okay?"

Marissa put her face back in the pillow as Julie yanked the nail out on two instead. As she wept and screamed into the sopped case, Julie gently put the nail on the nightstand and grabbed the hand again.

"Ready for the next one? The first one wasn't as bad as you thought, huh?"

Another grasp, another atrocious yank, and the feeling of warm stickiness running all over her fingers accompanied the blinding pain. Julie lined the second up next to the first and grabbed her hand again, but she no sooner grasped the nail of the middle finger than Marissa passed out cold.

∞

An hour later her eyes fluttered open. Julie was sitting in the chair in the corner, staring at her. "You slept through all of them but Zack's. Don't you even try it again. If you pass out, I'll dump rubbing alcohol all over your burns."

Julie got up and walked to the foot of the bed, where she took hold of Marissa's left foot. She was drowning in pain, all over her body, but now the throbbing in her hands and feet were excruciating, and she could feel sticky blood all over her.

"Only one more on this foot," Julie mumbled, almost to herself. "Then one more foot to go, and you will finally get some relief."

Another toenail was pulled, and Marissa began to scream for help, but she knew it was pointless. She began to beg, and even bargain. She promised as Julie set about grabbing the other foot, to turn herself in to the cops. She vowed to commit suicide. She offered the woman money, but there was no consolation for Julie Campbell. Marissa screamed and coughed as the last of the nails were pulled, then began to upchuck into the pillow. She knew she was going to die that day face down in the vomit-soaked pillow. As her last toe, the pinky on her right foot was raped of its protection and the skin that held it shredded from the force, Marissa lost consciousness.

R.W.K. Clark

# CHAPTER 29

"Wakey, wakey, baby killer," she taunted as she poked at the woman's blistered skin, even peeling pieces of it away for fun.

Marissa awoke immediately aware of the excruciating pain.

Julie went to the head of the bed and began trickling lighter fluid over the woman's hair. Then proceeded to cover Marissa's body with the remainder of the lighter fluid. It was afterward that she continued to push the four-poster bed to the already-opened window and struggled to position Marissa right next to it.

"This is not the way it is supposed to go," she said weakly. "I am the one who wins." Marissa heard the striking of a disposable lighter, and as the flame neared her head, she began to panic in earnest.

"Really?" Julie laughed.

Marissa slowly and painfully turned her head and looked Julie in the eye.

She touched the flame to Marissa's head, and as her hair went up like dry straw and her scalp started to blister. Without hesitation, Julie lit the rest of the woman aflame.

By the time Julie heard the sirens, she was already across the creek that ran along back and headed to her home.

# EPILOGUE

Julie was arrested later that day at her home, several miles out of Retribution. She was showered and clean, sitting in the living room, staring at the gas flame shooting around in the fireplace. Bobby stood by her side when they came, his hand on her shoulder. They had been waiting for their attorney to arrive for the last half-hour as soon as he called them and told them the police were on their way.

Fortunately, the court found her to be under such duress, coupled with the suspicion that Marissa Thomas was hurting children, and ruled that she should receive extensive therapy, pending further investigation.

One year later

Julie was legally discharged from court rule on a technicality; they were unable to place her at the scene of the crime. The cabbie was no help, he was so hopped up on energy drinks he didn't know which day was what. Finally, she was able to return home to her husband and their big, empty house.

Soon after, they decided to move to Comfort, Texas, to start anew. They purchased a black lab, and at first, Julie could hardly give him enough thanks for the hole the dog filled in her heart. But in eight more months, the couple decided to research adoption options, and it didn't take more than a year for the pain of Zack Campbell's wrongful death to slowly but surely sting a bit less.

Two years later

On the anniversary of Zack's death just two short years later, a woman with a fair amount of facial scarring stood up from a job interview and shook hands with a stout, bespectacled woman seated across from her.

"Thank you so much for the opportunity. I just know that I can contribute greatly to the families of Comfort."

"Well," the woman replied, "for a town this size, it is overrun with neglect and abuse. A worker of your stature is precisely what we have needed around here, may I call you Annie?"

"Yes, please."

She began to show the woman around the main social work area, introduce her co-workers, and show her where her workspace would be. Once there, the woman leaned in and, after a glance around, asked Annie a personal question.

"How many surgeries did you say you've had, Annie?"

She smiled. "Seven so far and I have six more to go. If you could have seen me after the house fire, you would be amazed at the progress. Luckily, I had a fire-retardant mattress. I'll bring photos. It's quite intriguing."

The woman smiled. "I'm sure. Anyway, I'm going to have you do casework on the phone, so your load will be slightly easier than you might have anticipated. Since you'll be starting today, go ahead and get comfortable. I'm going to run to my supervisor and grab your first cases."

Annie Thomas removed her light jacket and straightened the skirt of her business suit. Sitting down, she began to organize her desk.

Soon the woman was back. "Well, Annie, for the first month you'll focus on these three cases. At your thirty-day review, we will likely add more cases, but this should do until you get the ropes."

Annie smiled and continued to listen. "Now then, all you need to do with these first two cases is make two calls per week, speak to both the parents and children, and be sure to keep thorough notes on everything said, even the smallest word. Now, if you suspect anything unsavory, come to us, and we will send an investigative worker immediately, got it?"

"Absolutely. I will always be keeping my ears peeled."

"Now, the third one is actually adoption proceedings that were just begun last week. You will not need to visit the applicants right away. They have just entered the application process, and once they are approved, which could take months, or even a year or two, then we begin the visits. Pre-adoption interviews are conducted by the attending worker and I. If you are in good enough shape, you'll be there as well."

"Great!" Annie opened the first file. "I'm going to get reading up, and if I have any questions I can ask anyone?"

"Perfect," She gushed. "We'll check in on you later."

The first two files were the most interesting because they were about children neglected by junkie parents, and Annie found herself lost in the history. She was going to enjoy this job immensely. After a bit, she put the first two off to the side and opened the third. She nearly passed out when she read the names at the top of the application:

Bobby Campbell and Julie Campbell

With that, Annie threw her head back and laughed. She laughed so hard that she didn't even notice when her co-workers began to pop up their heads and look at her over the partition. She chuckled until the lady sidled up beside her and asked quietly, "Are you okay, Annie?"

As her laughter tapered off, she caught her breath, smiled and replied. "I'm just tickled about this job. You have made it too easy for me…"

# ENTREATY

This book was made possible by reviews from readers like you. Reviews fuel my creativity. If you enjoyed this novel, I implore you to please write a review and share your experience on the retailer's website. The livelihood for authors is entirely dependent on reviews, and I must say, it is the largest obstacle as a struggling author that I have encountered. Please tell a friend, tell a loved one about this read. With your help, I will be one step closer to overcoming this obstacle. In return, I thank you from the bottom of my heart, and sincerely appreciate your time and effort.

Humbled, with gratitude,

R.W.K. Clark

# ABOUT THE AUTHOR

I am a father of two beautiful children, Jon and Kim. They are my motivating forces; they are the lighthouse in this vast ocean. In my life, they are the air that I breathe; they are the oasis in this desert of uncertainty. They are my greatest joy in life and my number one priority. I have a long list of hobbies, and I attribute that to my lust for life! I like to surround myself with positive people, who share the same interests. Family values, the arts, outdoors, nature, and travel are tops on my list. I embrace attending cultural and artistic events because I believe dramatic self-expression is the window to the soul. I wear my heart on my sleeve, and I still believe in chivalry, and I always treat people the way I want to be treated.

www.rwkclark.com